DA
& FANCY

John Brosnan was born in Australia in 1947, but has lived in Britain for many years. He has written non-fiction books on the history of SF cinema, special effects and James Bond in the cinema. His novels include the *Sky Lords* trilogy and *The Opoponax Invasion*. *Damned and Fancy* is the first in a new series.

To Rob and Sarah

(serves you right)

DAMNED & FANCY

John Brosnan

LEGEND

Published in the United Kingdom in 1995 by Legend Books

1 3 5 7 9 10 8 6 4 2

First published in the United Kingdom in 1995 by

Legend Books
20 Vauxhall Bridge Road, London, SW1V 2SA

Random House Australia (Pty) Limited
20 Alfred Street, Milsons Point, Sydney,
New South Wales 2061, Australia

Random House New Zealand Limited
18 Poland Road, Glenfield
Auckland 10, New Zealand

Random House South Africa (Pty) Limited
PO Box 337, Bergvlei, South Africa

Random House UK Limited Reg. No. 954009

A CIP catalogue record for this book is available from the British Library

Papers used by Random House UK Limited are natural, recyclable products made from wood grown in sustainable forests. The manufacturing processes conform to the environmental regulations of the country of origin.

Printed and bound in Great Britain by Cox and Wyman

ISBN 0 09 951221 1

Chapter One

The demon farted, producing a flash of fire from under his tail and a sulphurous smell.

'Phew,' said Travis, waving his hand in front of his face. 'Did you have to?'

The demon, with a flutter of his leathery, black wings, resumed his perch on top of Whiplash's head. 'Sorry, but I couldn't help it. Shouldn't have had that second helping of goats' testicle stew.'

'Don't remind me.'

They were on a hill overlooking a grubby walled town. The mandatory castle stood in the centre of the town. It, too, appeared grubby, and the banners hanging limply from its spires looked as if they could do with a good wash. 'Doesn't look promising,' said Travis. 'Do you know what it's called?'

'Nope,' said the demon, whose name was Jack. 'I'm not a goddamned flying A to Z guide book.'

'Well, it doesn't matter. These places are all the same.' He dug his heels into Whiplash's sides. The horse snorted angrily. Travis dug his heels in again, harder. He wished he had spurs. Reluctantly, the horse started down the hill. Travis winced with each bump of the saddle. He'd been riding the stupid horse for several months now, but his bottom still hadn't become toughened to the continual mistreatment.

It was hot, and Travis was sweating profusely which made his coarsely-woven underwear even more itchy and uncomfortable than usual. He glanced up at the sun. He had estimated its diameter at one mile but it sure was a hot little bastard of a star.

They approached the town gate which was 'guarded' by two bored-looking soldiers wearing ragged uniforms and rusty helmets and breast-plates. Both men appeared to be in their early forties, were unshaven and had pot bellies protruding from beneath their breast-plates. They were armed with pikes and swords. Travis patted the Colt .45 automatic in the holster on his right hip, reassuring himself that it was still there, as he neared the two men. They regarded him and his demon with open suspicion. He brought Whiplash to a halt in front of them. 'Hello, lads,' he greeted them. 'Nice town you've got here.'

'It's not a town, it's a city,' said one of the guards, huffily.

'A *city*?' sneered Jack. 'You could have fooled me. So what's this *city* of yours called.'

'It's called Vallium,' said the other guard, glaring at Jack.

'Vallium?' repeated Travis, and laughed.

'What's so funny?' asked guard number one.

'Nothing really,' Travis said quickly. 'Vallium eh? Nice name.'

'What's your business here?' asked guard number two.

'I don't know yet,' Travis told him. 'I'm looking for work.'

'You'll be lucky to find any work in Vallium,' said number two. 'We're in a depression.'

'What kind of work do you do?'

'He's an aromatherapist,' said the demon.

'A what?' chorused one and two.

'Just Jack's rather sad idea of a joke. Actually I'm a sort of . . . how can I put this . . . a trouble-shooter.'

Two men regarded him with blank faces.

'Er . . . I help people out with their problems. For money.'

'Can you cure piles?' asked number two, hopefully.

Travis shook his head. 'Sorry, no. I don't mean problems like that.'

'So what sort of problems *do* you mean?' asked number one.

Travis said slowly, 'Well, say this town was suffering from a plague of thieves and cut-throats. I'd offer the authorities, for a price, my services and then er, remove the problem.'

'With my help,' muttered Jack.

'Oh yes, with Jack's help.'

'Crime rate is real low in Vallium,' said number two.

'King's a strict bastard. But we do have a plague of rats. You do rats?'

'No. Rats aren't my scene. I do *dragons*, though.'

The two guards exchanged a glance. Then number one said to Travis, 'Well, it just so happens we do have a dragon problem these days. A serious one.'

Travis grinned broadly. 'I've come at just the right time, then!'

They looked him up and down. 'No offence, squire, but you don't look much of a dragon-fighter,' said number one. 'And that pig-sticker hanging from your belt wouldn't be of any use against *our* dragon. He's the size of a barn. He can fry a man at fifty yards. We've had all sorts of so-called dragon-slayers turning up here to deal with him. Full of dragon-fighting references as long as your arm until it's burnt off.'

'Ah, but I have hidden talents,' said Travis.

'You a sorcerer?' asked number one, breaking the pattern of their routine.

'If only. No, I'm not a sorcerer. Now may I enter?'

They both shook their heads.

'Why not?'

'You could by a spy,' said number one. 'Be more than our jobs' worth if we let you in and you turned out to be a spy. The King would stick our heads on the castle battlements.'

'Aye,' agreed number two, 'and we'd lose our pensions, too.'

'I'm not a spy,' said Travis.

'Well, you *would* say that, wouldn't you? Can you prove it?'

Travis sighed and asked, 'Who would I be spying *for*? Is Vallium at war with anyone?'

'Well, no,' admitted number two.

'So how could I possibly be a spy?'

They didn't answer. Jack said, 'The key to the city is in your money pouch, Travis.'

'Oh,' said Travis as he realized what the demon meant. He loosened the draw string and reached into his pouch. Five coins jingled at its bottom. He took out two half sovereigns and tossed one each to the two guards. He was left with a mere two sovereigns and one quarter-sovereign. Things were getting desperate. Goats' testicle stew loomed ominously in his future.

After biting the coins, the two guards saluted him. 'Welcome to Vallium, squire,' said number one. 'Enjoy your stay, sir,' said number two.

'Thank you. Could either of you direct me to a good inn? A good *cheap* inn?'

'To be sure, sir,' said number two. 'Just follow the main road to the town square. There's an inn right by the gibbet. Can't miss it. Has a sign saying "The Inn" on the front of it.'

'Is it cheap?'

Number two shrugged. 'It's run by my uncle, and if you tell him I sent you he'll be sure to give you a discount.'

'And you are . . . ?' asked Travis.

'Claude.'

'Well, thank you, Claude, I'll certainly do that.' He kicked Whiplash in the ribs and, with a snort of annoyance, the horse moved through the gate.

Vallium, on closer inspection, lived up to its name. The architecture, and the people in the streets, looked dull. Jack, echoing Travis's thoughts, said, 'Dullsville is right.'

'Doesn't look too prosperous either.'

'The money will be in the castle, as usual,' muttered Jack.

They arrived in the town square and found the inn – right by the gibbet which was, mercifully, unoccupied. Travis dismounted and led Whiplash to the large stable attached to the side of the inn. A burly, balding man, wearing a dirty apron, was tossing hay with a pitchfork into an empty stall. 'Hello! Know where I can find the inn-keeper?' Travis asked.

The man stopped working, leaned on the pitchfork and looked Travis up and down, spat onto the straw and followed with a copious amount of mucus from his nose. Then he said, wiping his nose, 'Right here. Bulric's the name.'

Hoping that the spitting and nose-blowing routine wasn't part of some obligatory greeting ritual, Travis said, 'A profound pleasure to meet you, Bulric. I'm Travis. Your nephew, Claude, recommended your establishment. I need a room for a couple of nights, and stable space and feed for my horse.'

Bulric spat again on the straw-covered floor. 'Don't allow demons in the inn. It'll have to stay out here with the horse.'

'Racist bastard,' muttered Jack.

'What yer say?' said Bulric, glaring at Jack.

'Nothing,' said Travis quickly. 'The stable will be fine for him. How much for the two nights?'

'Yer be requiring food?'

'Very much so. What's on the menu?'

'Menu?' repeated Bulric.

'I mean, What Are You Serving Today?' said Travis.

'Oh. Well, there's pigeon soup and bread to start, followed by today's special . . .'

Travis tensed, waiting for the dreaded words: 'goats' testicle stew'. But instead he heard Bulric say, to his relief:

'. . . steak and potatoes, and all the ale you can drink.'

'Marvellous' cried Travis. 'Now the matter of payment . . .'

Bulric scratched his chin, 'Two sovereigns in all, squire.'

Travis winced, and handed the landlord his two remaining sovereigns. 'How much would it have been if I hadn't been sent by your nephew?'

'One and a half sovereigns.'

'I don't understand. That's *less* than I paid! What about the discount?'

Bulric spat on the ground again. 'No discount. If that shite of a nephew of mine thinks he can get in my good books by sending me custom he'll soon learn it's a waste of time. I'll charge the poor bastards extra.'

Travis was about to argue that it wasn't *his* fault he'd ignorantly stumbled into a family squabble but realized it would probably be useless. Jack gave him a nasty laugh and rustled his wings.

'When you've got yer horse and yer flying pet rat settled go into the kitchen there . . .' He pointed at a side door,

'. . . and introduce yerself to the girl, Helen. She'll take care of yer needs. Hor, hor.'

'Thanks.' Travis wondered just what taking care of his needs would entail. He led Whiplash into a stall, and while the horse began munching about in a crudely built manger full of oats he stripped off the saddle, saddle blanket and harness and gave the horse a brisk grooming. Jack hopped down the horse's neck and onto its back. 'Damn, I'm hungry,' he said.

'I'll bring you some scraps when I'm through eating. God, steak and potatoes! I can't wait.'

'I'd have preferred goats' testicle stew.'

'That's because you're sick and twisted. Now stay here and behave yourself.'

The demon gave him a mocking bow. 'Yes, oh Great One. Your word is my command.'

'Don't overdo the sarcasm, shorty. You might drown in it,' Travis told him.

As Travis headed for the kitchen he wished he could get rid of the odious Jack. However, he knew the demon had been assigned to be his adviser and helper in this world, known as Samella, and though he'd been here for many months now he still relied heavily on the bugger's services and advice. Without Jack, his survival was doubtful. So he was just going to have to put up with the little monster . . . Shit.

He entered the kitchen, and was hit by the overpowering smell of either cooking food or boiling laundry. He couldn't tell which. A plumpish girl with red hair sat on a stool by a large metal pot, resting on a glowing grill, giving it a desultory stir with a long wooden spoon. Travis saw that she was quite pretty and couldn't help admiring the vista of ample breasts that her very low-cut dress revealed. 'You Helen?' he asked.

She smiled at him as she rose from the stool. 'Yessir, I am.'

Pity about the teeth, he thought. 'Your father said you'd show me to my room and, well, look after me . . .'

She giggled. 'Bulric, my father? What a bloody thought!'

'Oh, I'm sorry, I just assumed . . .'

'Bulric's not even married: He prefers boys in his bed, does Bulric, not women!' And she laughed even harder.

He waited patiently, then said, 'Bulric mentioned hot food – a *steak* to be exact – and ale.'

She wiped her eyes. 'Yessir. I'll take you to your room first and then I'll bring you dinner.'

She led him up a flight of creaky, straw-strewn wooden stairs, along a passageway and into a large room with a window overlooking the town square. Looking round he saw a big bed, a table, two chairs and a crude structure that he assumed was meant to be a wardrobe. The bed consisted of a big, low box containing a rough hessian mattress from which straw protruded. On the end of the bed lay what appeared to Travis to be a primitive duvet, made of coarse linen and also stuffed with straw. Not for the first time it occurred to him that straw was this world's major product.

'I'll just go and put your steak on the grill, sir. Shouldn't take long.' She hurried from the room. If Travis had been capable of laughing hollowly, he would have.

He sat on the bed, pulled off his boots and massaged his feet. Moving over to the window, he pushed the two heavy shutters and stared out across the square. A crowd seemed to be forming on the opposite side. Then there was a brief knock on the door. It opened. It was the girl again. She gave him a smile and walked over to the bed. He was taken by surprise when she flung herself backwards onto the bed and lay there in a pose of studied abandonment. 'And what about you, sir? You're not like Bulric, are you?'

'Pardon?'

'You don't prefer boys in your bed to girls?' she said, smiling enticingly at him. The teeth definitely spoiled the overall effect, but now he knew for sure what Bulric had meant when he'd said that Helen would take care of all his needs. On the other hand, were her services included in the overall charge or was she an extra? One ought to know these things.

She said, 'You're a good-looking fellow, sir, and I'd gladly pleasure you for free but Bulric insists he and I split fifty-fifty, so . . .'

He sighed. 'How much?'

'Half a sovereign.'

'Oh.'

Mistaking the reason for his hesitancy she slowly pulled her dress up to her waist.

She wasn't wearing any underwear, which came as no surprise to Travis. Underwear had yet to catch on in a big way in Samella and considering how uncomfortable the available product was, it was perfectly understandable. He gazed at her luxuriant growth of matching red hair and told her, a little wistfully, that he only had a quarter of a sovereign.

She looked thoughtful for a few moments, smiled, and said, 'Alright, a quarter will do. That'll keep Bulric satisfied. Just make sure you do the same for me. Now hurry up before that steak starts to burn.'

He hurried out of his clothes, not easy as the clothes weren't designed to be hurried out of, and joined Helen on the bed. He helped her get her dress up over her head. She smelt ripe but he expected her to. And besides, he guessed he smelt ripe as well.

He soon had any thought of cooking completely out of her mind.

Since arriving in Samella, Travis had quickly discovered he had a distinct advantage over other men here. It was his knowledge of sophisticated sexual techniques – such as foreplay. He felt much like a Frenchman must have done in Australia during the nineteen fifties.

When it was finally over she lay there gasping and said, 'By the horned gods of Zelpit, no man's ever done *that* to me before!'

'Really?' he said, with contrived innocence.

'No, never! And I've had more men than I can count!'

Travis thought this was clearly an understatement. If she

could have counted past ten he would have been very surprised.

'You're not from these parts are you?' she panted.

'No, I'm not,' he said, truthfully.

'Do all the men in your country pleasure women the same way as you do?'

'Um, I *think* so, but it all depends on which part of the country you're in, and how much they've had to drink.'

She guffawed and gave his limp penis a painful tweak. 'You silly fool!'

'Ouch,' he said, pushing her hand away and sitting up. It was then he became aware of the sound of angry voices coming through the open window. 'What's going on out there?' he asked.

She bounded up off the bed and bounced towards the window, her large pink bottom wobbling affectingly. He followed, and leaned on the sill beside her. On the opposite side of the square the crowd of people he'd seen earlier were now surrounding a coach and horses. A man stood on the coach and even from a distance Travis could tell he was dressed in finery. He was gesticulating at the crowd. 'Who's that?' he asked Helen as he ran an appreciative hand over her bottom.

'Oh, it's the Chancellor. He's asking for another delay for Princess Beatrice, but the people aren't going to sit still for it this time. Beatrice is going to end up dragon fodder for sure.'

'Who is Princess Beatrice?'

'The bleeding King's bleeding daughter. So far she's ducked her fate whenever her name has been pulled out of the hat.'

'I'm a stranger here, remember,' he told her. 'What are you talking about? And what's the dragon got to do with it?'

She gave him an impatient look. 'It's the usual dragon deal. Garaptor – that's the dragon – has promised not to destroy the town in return for a virgin maiden being handed into his horrible clutches once a month. Trouble is, we're running out of virgins. We're down to our last one. Princess Beatrice . . .'

'I see.'

'The selection was made by lottery,' continued Helen. 'And when Beatrice's name has been picked before, the King and the Chancellor have bribed men to offer their own daughters in her place. But that won't work now. Like I said: no more virgins.' She turned from the window and went and picked up her dress.

'What happens next month, then?' Travis asked. 'When you won't have a single virgin to offer whats-its-name?'

'Garaptor. Bloody Hell. Oh, once he's used up all the virgins he'll leave us in peace. That's the deal. I reckon that Princess Beatrice is the one he's really been after all along.' She headed for the door. 'I'll go fetch your dinner.'

Deep in thought, Travis began to get dressed. A rustle of leathery wings made him turn. Jack was landing on the window-sill. 'Been having fun, I see,' the demon said with a sneer. 'I suppose you blew the last of our money on that silly cow.'

'*My* money, yes, but it was worth it. By this time tomorrow I'll be rich.'

The demon produced a pack of Marlboro from a pouch in its stomach, drew out a cigarette, blew on its tip to light it and then began to smoke it. 'This should be good. So spill.'

Travis told Jack about Princess Beatrice versus the dragon. '. . . So I slay the dragon, return the Princess to her father, and he'll gratefully shower me with more gold than I can carry without risking a double hernia. End of story.'

Jack blew three smoke rings into the air. They were linked. 'End of *fairy* story, you mean. You haven't even *seen* a dragon, much less killed one. Dragons have thick, scaly hides. That pea-shooter of yours . . .' He pointed the cigarette at the .45 that lay in its holster on the floor, '. . . won't even put a small dent in a dragon.'

'I'll aim for its eyes,' said Travis, with a forced confidence, 'I've become a pretty good shot since I arrived here.' It went very quiet.

'Can't argue with you on that, but you'll still have to get pretty damn close to take out one of its eyes with a pistol shot . . . and by that time you'll be a walking kebab.'

Frowning, Travis rubbed his chin. 'You have a point, Jack.'

'Yeah, and that's apart from the one on the end of my tail. Ha, ha, ha.'

'I'll have to come up with an idea. Something really cunning.'

'If you were capable of being really cunning you wouldn't be here in the first place,' said the demon, and laughed. Then he hurriedly stubbed out the cigarette on the windowsill and rose into the air with a flutter of his wings. 'Someone's coming. Must fly.'

Jack disappeared from view just as the door opened. It was Helen. She was carrying a wooden tray on which a large bowl of food steamed enticingly.

'Ah!' cried Travis. 'My steak!'

She shook her head. 'Sorry, that got burned right through while I was bein' pleasured up here by you.'

'So what's that then?' he asked suspiciously.

'All we had left in the kitchen . . . goats' testicle stew.'

Travis made his firm decision then and there. That dragon was dead meat.

Chapter Two

When, some months in the past, Travis Thomson had woken up in a leafy glade and found he was wearing blue tights and a bright red cod-piece he'd instinctively known that something wasn't quite right. He'd slowly sat up, aware that his head ached and he was very thirsty, and looked around. Standing nearby in the leafy glade was a sad-eyed horse chewing, in a morose fashion, on the long grass. Perched on the horse's saddle was what appeared to Travis to be a large black bat. The fact that it was smoking a cigarette was something he'd put aside for the time being.

He looked down at himself. Apart from the tights and the cod-piece he was wearing a yellow leather jacket, a red cape, black gloves and long, black boots. He felt his head. Some sort of cap – with a curly feather – was sitting on it. He was also wearing a thick belt from which hung a sword and scabbard on the right, and a gun in a holster on his left side. A pouch and dagger hung next to the sword. Panic welled up within him. He tried telling himself to calm down but himself wouldn't listen. Then, more forcibly, he told himself that there was a rational explanation for all this. It was then that the 'bat' spoke . . .

'In case you're wondering where you are, pal, and I'm sure you are, you're in deep shit.'

Travis stared at the 'bat' in horror. Panic no longer welled within him: it had become a geyser. 'Arghhhhh,' he croaked.

'Yeah, it's a bitch, isn't it?' said the bat, though by now Travis could see it wasn't a bat after all. It had a human-like face, horns, arms as well as wings and a long, pointed tail. And the accent of its gravelly voice was distinctly American.

'Arghhhhh,' Travis croaked again. His mind had given up seeking a rational explanation. He wanted his mother. Immediately.

The thing gave a sigh, reached down and grabbed one of the two canteens that hung from the saddle. 'Here, catch,' it told Travis, tossing the canteen towards him. Travis automatically caught it.

'Gwerrärh?'

'It's brandy. Take a *big* swig. You need it. Then we can talk.'

Travis stared suspiciously at the canteen he was holding.

'Hey, trust me,' said the thing. 'It's just brandy, really.'

Travis numbly pulled the cork from the canteen and sniffed the contents. It certainly smelt like brandy. He put the canteen to his mouth and drank. It was brandy, alright. It burnt the back of his throat and made his eyes water, but the warmth that spread through him felt good. He looked at the thing again. 'Thanks,' he muttered.

'You're welcome, Travis,' it said, then held up a clawed hand. 'Yeah, I know your name. I know a lot about you. Oh, I'm Jack, by the way.'

The brandy had reached his head. Suddenly, that didn't seem high enough. He took another big swallow. The edge was already gone from his panic. Travis was beginning to feel, well, *better* about everything. He was also starting to believe that he was having some kind of incredibly lucid *lurid* dream. It was the only possible explanation.

'Err, *Jack*,' he said to the thing, 'I don't want to be rude, but just what exactly *are* you?'

'I'm a demon,' it told him, and blew a series of linked smoke rings from its cigarette.

'Oh,' said Travis. He glanced around the glade. It seemed to be midday and the sun was hot. And it all looked so real. He noticed details like the bees that hovered around the various types of wild flowers. A large butterfly with beautiful wings soared into the glade but, when it got closer, he saw that it wasn't a butterfly but a fairy. A female fairy. It was nude and had tiny, dainty breasts. She flew once around his head, made a high-pitched sound and then fluttered out of the glade.

'I wasn't always a demon,' said the demon. 'Back home in LA I was a movie producer.'

'Really? How interesting,' said Travis politely.

'Yeah, I'm Jack DeSolva,' the demon said proudly. 'You heard of me?'

'Uh . . . no, I don't think so.' He drank more of the brandy.

'Maybe you've seen some of my movies? *The Night of the Long Scream*? *Slimer*? *Sex School for Horror*? *The De-Frocking*? They all did great on video.'

Travis shook his head. 'No, sorry.'

'You amaze me. Okay, so I wasn't a Spielberg or anything but I had a big cult following. Still do, I bet. Used to do lectures at colleges about my early days in the industry. How I started out with Roger Corman and stuff like that.'

'Uh-huh,' said Travis, encouragingly, even though he hadn't heard of Roger Corman either.

'Yeah, I was doing well until I got mixed up with . . . *him*. I tried to pull a fast one . . . And *he* did this to me.' The demon shuddered.

Travis was now aware that he felt very itchy. Whatever underwear he had on seemed to be woven out of the bristles of a toilet brush. And talking about toilets . . .

Jack maliciously stubbed out his cigarette on the horse's rump. The horse jerked, turned its head and whinnied in protest. 'Ah, shut up, you dumb nag,' said the demon. To Travis, he said, 'His name is Whiplash, if you're interested.'

'The man who turned you into a demon?' asked Travis.

'No, the *horse*, you idiot. The bastard who did this to me, and the guy who stuck you in this place, is Prenderghast. Gideon Leonard Prenderghast.'

Travis was staggered. 'Prenderghast? What's Prenderghast got to do with this?'

'Everything. What's the last thing you remember?'

'I . . . I'm not sure.' He remembered going to his office, talking to his editor about the story he was working on – the Prenderghast story – and then . . . it was all a blank.

'Try harder.'

And then it came to him. 'I was talking to Prenderghast, in his penthouse office in the Docklands. Well, it was more of a confrontation, I guess. I was telling him what I'd found out about his operation . . . and all the things I *hadn't* found out about him. That he had *no* traceable background . . . He began to get angry . . . very angry . . . and . . .' Travis rubbed his forehead. 'No, I can't remember anything else.'

'You pissed him. Like I did. That's why you're here.'

'Do you *really* mean that Prenderghast is responsible for me being . . .' Travis gestured at the surrounding glade, '. . . here. Where exactly *is* here?'

'That's kind of difficult to explain,' said the demon. 'For a start, this world is called Samella . . .'

'I'm supposed to be on a different *planet*?'

'Pal, you aren't just on a different planet, you're in an entirely different goddamned *universe*. And things here don't work the way you're used to.' He pointed upwards. 'Like the sun there. This world doesn't revolve around it, *it* revolves around this world. There's lots of stuff like that.'

'I see,' said Travis, not seeing anything at all. 'And how did Prenderghast manage to send me here?'

The demon shrugged, produced a packet of Marlboro and lit another cigarette. 'He can do 'most anything he damn well wants. He has The Power. He's kinda like a sorcerer, but he's much more than that. And, pal, he's *definitely* not human.'

Travis had had enough. 'This is preposterous!' he exploded. 'He's just a computer-toy manufacturer! He makes virtual reality games for kids! That's what I was investigating him about . . . the reported cases of his VR head-sets having a bad effect on children . . .' Travis ran down. He remembered the expression of growing rage on the fat man's face as he'd rattled off his chain of accusations: the possible harmful neurological side-effects caused by the use of Prenderghast's head-sets; the wide-spread psychological damage caused by getting countless children hooked on his banal sword-and-sorcery virtual reality scenarios . . .

And then a bulb switched on above his head. 'I get it now! I know what's going on here!'

'You do?' said the demon, sounding a little surprised.

'*Prenderghast* is doing this to me!'

'I just told you that, you dope.'

'Prenderghast has got me wired into some fucking enormous sophisticated virtual reality system! He's trying to teach me a lesson. Hell, what am I saying? *You're* probably Prenderghast yourself, talking to me through that little monstrosity of a demon you've cooked up. (Jack looked hurt.) Well, okay, Mister Prenderghast, you've had your fun and made your point, now turn this thing off and put me back in the real world . . .'

The demon shook his head sadly, stretched his wings and flew into the air. Before Travis could react, Jack flew straight at him and whipped his barbed tail across Travis's face. The pain was searing.

'Ow!' Travis cried, shocked. He put his hand to his cheek, then looked at his fingers. They were spattered with blood. The demon, meanwhile, returned to its former roosting spot on the horse's saddle.

'Still think this place isn't real?'

'That *hurt*!' said Travis, in wonderment.

'It was supposed to,' said the demon, flicking the stub of his cigarette into the grass.

'I don't see how . . . unless . . . my God, you've somehow hooked your system directly into my pain centres! I didn't know that VR technology had gone this far!'

'Shit,' said the demon, with a sigh.

'Right, stop all this immediately, Prenderghast!' demanded Travis, getting to his feet. 'I've got a dinner date at seven pm. I made reservations at the Red Fort. Heather will be furious if I'm late again.'

'Listen, dickbrain, forget your dinner date. I am not that bastard Prenderghast, I am Jack DeSolva, former Hollywood producer of cheap but tasteful exploitation movies and now stuck here as a damned demon, thanks to Prenderghast! And you are not – I repeat – *not* in some virtual reality fantasy world! This place is just as real as back home!'

'I can't believe that,' protested Travis, as he approached the demon and the horse. 'Not for a minute. This *has* to be some sort of VR illusion.'

'Suit yourself, pal,' the demon told him. 'You'll just have to learn the hard way. This world is real: here you can get hurt, get sick, get yourself killed, or starve to death if you don't eat. And you may notice that money pouch on your belt only contains a few coins. When they run out you're going to need some more. In other words, get a job. *Capisce*?'

'A job?'

'Yeah. And *my* job is to act as your little pal, to teach you the ropes. Prenderghast wouldn't like it if you got killed on your first day here. No fun for him in that.'

Travis was feeling unsure again. It *had* to be a trick of some kind but the damned demon sounded so matter-of-fact. He looked around the glade. Trees as far as he could see. Bird sounds. Maybe Prenderghast had drugged him, taken him to some forest. And now he was trying to freak him out with this talking demon. Travis stared at the demon. Maybe it was an animatronic model . . . operated by remote control. Yeah, and the fairy had been a very, very *small* animatronic model . . .

Sure. The only problem with that theory was that England had been in the middle of a particularly bitter winter and yet this was clearly a hot, summer's day. Had Prenderghast gone to the time and trouble of flying him to a different country? Or – horror of horrors – was Jack telling the truth? Nah.

'You're stuck here indefinitely, pal,' said the demon. 'Unless you find the Key. And that, I'm told, is pretty unlikely.'

'Key? What Key?'

The demon shrugged. 'Haven't a clue. Prenderghast didn't tell me. But he said you'd know it if you ever found it.'

Travis groaned. 'Are you telling me I'm supposed to go on some damned *quest*?'

'Sounds like it. In between jobs you look for the Key.' He lit another cigarette and blew smoke into Travis's face.

'What kind of jobs?'

'Depends what you're good at.'

'I'm a journalist. That's what I'm good at.'

The demon shook his head. 'Strike one, pal. No newspapers here. You could start one up, I suppose, but distribution would be a bastard. And anyway, not many people here can read more than a few basic words.'

'So what could I do?'

'I hear you know how to use that.' The demon pointed at the sword hanging by his side.

'Yes, I fenced at college.' He drew the sword. It was a rapier, like a stronger version of a foil. 'How did you know?'

'Prenderghast, of course.'

How had Prenderghast known that, Travis wondered? Unless he'd done a lot of checking up on him. He swished the sword back and forth through the air, noting that it was well-balanced.

'A good swordsman is always in plenty of demand in this place,' said the demon, and cackled suggestively. 'You'll get action, with my help.'

Travis returned the sword to its scabbard and then drew the automatic pistol . . .

'Hey, careful with that thing!' cried the demon. 'It's loaded.'

He hefted the gun in his hand. It was heavy. 'Why do they need swords here if they've got guns?' he asked.

'*They* don't have guns. Just you. Prenderghast figured you'd last a bit longer with an edge.'

'Oh.' Travis stared at the automatic. 'Is there any spare ammunition?'

'You don't need it. The clip will never run out.' The demon laughed and added, 'You got a *magic* gun there, pal. Like my pack of Marlboro.' He lit another cigarette.

Travis put the gun back in the holster. 'I'm flattered. But right now I have something more pressing to worry about.'

'Which is?'

'I need a toilet, badly. Are there any in the vicinity?'

The demon chuckled again – so hard he nearly fell off the horse.

'I'll take that as a "no" then,' said Travis sourly.

Chapter Three

Travis squatted over the hole that led to the cess pit beneath the rear of the inn and wondered what was happening back in the real world. What did his family and friends think had happened to him? Had they given up hope of seeing him again? Had he been fired from the magazine in his absence? Had fickle Heather gone back to her former boyfriend, Brian? Probably. After all, it had been over five months now and he doubted if Heather had ever gone without sex for that length of time. At least, not since she'd turned sixteen, which was when, she'd once told him, she'd become sexually active. And that was . . . how long ago? Good grief, he couldn't remember how old she was. Twenty-six, or twenty-seven? Or was it twenty-eight?

He was getting worried about his memory. Details about the real world were starting to fade. Gaps – small ones so far – were appearing in his memory. He was worried that eventually *this* place would seem more real to him than reality. Maybe that was Prenderghast's intention: to drive him nutty by a prolonged link-up with his damned virtual reality system.

Travis believed, much of the time, that Samella was some incredibly sophisticated computer generation but he had learned to *treat* it as if it was real. He had no choice. As far as his brain was concerned it *was* real. As the demon had warned, here he felt things like pain and hunger just as keenly as in the real world. And because conditions were so primitive in this backward society he was suffering far more discomfort than he'd ever done back in reality.

For example, *this*, he thought grimly as he scooped up a handful of straw from the floor around him. If only Prenderghast had exiled him to a world where they'd invented indoor plumbing and toilet paper . . .

Travis hoped that Prenderghast was taking good care of his real body while it was hooked up into the state-of-the-art computer system. Five months was a long time to be comatose. His muscles would be atrophying and he might, by now, be a mass of bed-sores. Then again, he couldn't be sure that time was passing in the real world at the same rate that it appeared to be passing here. Maybe it was like a dream in the early morning when you're slipping in and out of sleep. You could build Rome in the dream but when you woke up again and glanced at the clock only a minute or so had actually gone by. Maybe he'd only been linked up to Prenderghast's machine for an hour or so . . . maybe he would even make it to dinner with Heather at the Red Fort on time . . . And maybe Michelle Pfeiffer would be waiting back in his room wearing a very small, black leather bikini.

He sighed, got to his feet, pulled up his tights and adjusted his cod-piece. He returned to his room. No Michelle Pfeiffer. Just Jack, who was picking through the remains on Travis's breakfast tray. 'Help yourself,' he said to the demon as he sat on the edge of the bed and began putting on his boots.

'I am,' said the demon as nibbled on something that Travis hadn't been able to identify. 'Worked out your strategy for rescuing the Princess yet?'

'Well, not exactly. I came up with something while I was having breakfast . . .'

'Was it this?' asked Jack, brandishing another unidentifiable item of food.

Travis ignored him. 'I asked Helen what the drill was with the sacrificial virgin routine. All the sacrifices take place in a disused rock quarry about eight miles to the north of the town. The victim is escorted out there by a bunch of soldiers and a band . . .'

The demon stopped eating. 'A band? A band of what?'

'A *musical* band. Apparently they play "Come and get it" type music to alert the dragon. Anyway, the victim gets chained to a post and the escort high-tail it out of the quarry as fast as they can . . .'

'What about the band? Does it play on during the meal? Like in a restaurant?'

Travis sighed. 'No, Jack. The band goes too. That just leaves the poor virgin with only a white, sacrificial negligee between herself and ten tons of mean, hungry dragon.'

'So what was your plan?'

Travis pulled the gun out of its holster, removed the ammunition clip and checked it. It was full, as usual, but he couldn't stop himself from making sure. 'Well, I thought I'd get there before they all arrived and hide myself near the post. When the escort – and the band – has gone I'll free the Princess and take her place.'

Jack laughed. 'Look, dickwit, dragons might tend to be near-sighted but even one with a white stick would be able to see that you're no virgin princess.'

'I'm going to be disguised, of course. With a wig. And I was going to exchange clothes with the princess . . .' His voice faltered.

'As much as I'd enjoy seeing you wearing a sacrificial negligee, that is the stupidest plan I've ever heard,' said Jack. 'Hell, even Roger Corman wouldn't touch a plot like that.'

'Yeah, it does have a few weak points, doesn't it?' agreed Travis. 'The time factor, for a start . . .'

'Not to mention the dickwit factor.'

'But I've got to get close enough for a head-shot, somehow. It's my only chance.'

The demon scratched its arse. Or, as he referred to it, ass. 'Maybe there'll be a place you can hide real close to the munching post. I say we should ride out now and check that quarry over.'

'Good idea . . .'

There was a knock on the door, and Helen entered without waiting for a response. She gave Jack a disapproving glare. He winked at her and licked his lips.

'If Bulric catches you in here there'll be the devil to pay,' she told Jack as she shooed him off the breakfast tray. He flew up and landed on one of the ceiling beams, from where he leered down at Helen. 'What a fine body of a woman, eh Travis? But then you know that already.'

Helen turned her glare on Travis as she picked up the tray. 'What you been telling that flying piece of demonic filth?' she demanded.

'Nothing, nothing at all. It's just his naturally dirty mind. Now, that quarry you were telling me about . . . is there any chance of you drawing me a rough map of how I get there?'

She gave him a hard look. 'You're going to try and rescue Princess Beatrice, aren't you. That's what all those questions was about.'

'Maybe,' he admitted. 'It all depends.'

She went *tsk tsk*. 'Be a real waste of a man if you do. A real waste.' She headed for the door.

'Hey, a little bit of support wouldn't go amiss, you know.' he cried.

'You'll need more than a cod-piece to help you with Garaptor,' she said as she left.

Travis was lying, under a layer of leaves, in a shallow depression between some rocks. He was hot, sticky and very uncomfortable but he had to admit it made an ideal hiding place, since it was only ten yards from the sacrificial virgin launching pad. Jack and Whiplash were hidden in a grove of trees about a half a mile from the quarry.

As Travis lay there getting cramps he wondered what the time was. Not having a watch was another major inconvenience of this damned world. He estimated he'd been there for at least an hour. Helen had told him that midday was the traditional time for offering the dragon its lunch. That left him another half hour to wait.

He raised his head slightly and peered through his covering of leaves towards the sacrificial stake that stood in a patch of cleared ground. The area showed signs of having been repeatedly scorched, and littered about the stake were several bones. Human bones. Travis shivered. He had asked Jack on more than one occasion what would happen to him if he got killed in this world but the demon had refused to answer. Instead he had just chuckled nastily each time.

Suddenly he heard the pitter-patter of tiny feet. Glancing around worriedly, he saw a small, bulbous figure hurrying by. A goblin. And it was carrying a knife and fork. Travis watched as it disappeared down a hole not far from the stake. He wondered what that unpleasant little creature was doing there. Then he realized what the knife and fork were for. The goblin was apparently hoping to get the left-overs . . .

Suddenly Travis heard distant snatches of music. Well, no: *music* was a bit strong. More accurately, it was the sound made by primitive wind and percussion instruments being profoundly abused. This was apparently the signal to the dragon that lunch was on its way. As the procession drew closer, and the noise louder, Travis wondered why Garaptor hadn't eaten the band rather than the offered virgin. It would have been far more merciful for all concerned.

Travis peered cautiously towards the entrance of the quarry. The 'band' appeared first, its members staring anxiously upwards as they continued to torture their instruments. They were followed by six armoured men on horseback holding lances from which frayed banners fluttered limply. Behind them came an expensive-looking carriage drawn by four horses, and behind that appeared a motley group of foot soldiers. The latter were also casting nervous glances towards the sky.

The rag-bag procession reached the sacrificial stake and formed a circle around it. The band kept up the awful noise while a footman jumped down from the carriage, opened the door and helped a small fat man, dressed in regal robes, alight. He immediately waved his arms about in an angry fashion and the 'music' died thankfully away. The King, for it was clearly he, then helped someone else down from the carriage: a young woman wearing a long black cloak. And this, thought Travis, had to be Princess Beatrice.

He regarded her with mounting interest as the King led her to the stake. His first impression was that she was straight out of a fairy tale. She had an angelic, ethereal beauty. She was like Disney's Snow White but drawn by better artists. And when the King, muttering apologies, removed her cloak, Travis exclaimed to himself, 'Wow, Snow White with *boobs*!' The sheer, clinging white sacrificial gown revealed that Princess Beatrice's body rated a '10' in any world, real or unreal.

The King kept up his string of apologies as he shackled his daughter to the stake. She maintained an aloof silence, though her expression clearly showed her opinion of her father. Finally he cried, 'Please say something, my dear. You have no idea the pain this is causing me . . .'

'I'll try and keep that in mind when Garaptor is chewing on my limbs,' she said at last, her beautiful voice dripping with contempt.

One of the knights dismounted, with difficulty, and went over to the Princess and her father. He dropped shakily to one knee with a clank and squeal of metal in front of the Princess and lifted his visor. It squealed too. 'Your Highness,' he said to the Princess, 'You know I'd give anything to remain here with you and face Garaptor but your father has forbidden me that honour.'

She looked down with disdain at the kneeling knight, 'Oh, shut your visor, Rodney. If you were a real man you'd disobey this doddering old hypocrite and try and save my life.'

'Beatrice!' cried the King in a shocked tone.

'Your Highness, you know I can't break my sacred vows to your father, the King,' said the knight.

'And what about the promises you made *me*?' the Princess asked angrily. 'If you'd kept at least one of them you'd have deflowered me in the north tower last week and I wouldn't be in this bloody mess!'

'Beatrice!' cried the King again, sounding even more shocked. And then, turning to the knight, 'Sir Rodney!'

'Don't worry, father,' said the Princess, 'Sir Rodney never showed up. Your threat to execute any man who deflowered me by having hot lead poured into his rectum seemed to have the desired effect. Funny how preserving my virginity means more to your sense of honour than preserving my life!'

'My dear, you just don't understand these things . . .'

'Excuse me!' called one of the other knights. 'Don't mean to interrupt or anything, Your Highness, but shouldn't we be getting a move on?'

'What?' said the King, who looked up at the sky. 'Oh, yes, you're right.' He gave the Princess a quick kiss on the cheek. 'Chin up, dear. The kingdom will never forget your sacrifice. Give my regards to your mother if you come across her in the next world. Bye bye.' He hurried back to his carriage and was helped inside by the footman. Sir Rodney rose, with difficulty, to his feet. 'Beatrice. . .' he said helplessly.

'Oh, drop dead, Rodney,' she said and looked away.

He went reluctantly to his horse and, with immense effort, remounted. Led by the King's carriage, and with Sir Rodney bringing up the rear, the procession departed from the quarry at a gathering pace. And then all was quiet.

Princess Beatrice pulled experimentally on the chains shackled to her wrists. She muttered, 'Pissy bollocks.'

Travis wanted to call to her, to reassure her that she wasn't alone, but he didn't dare reveal his presence. The element of surprise was the only advantage he had. Apart from the .45. He drew the latter from its holster and cocked it as quietly as he could. Even so, the princess heard the sound and looked in his direction. 'Is someone there?' she asked.

'*Shit!*' he muttered and buried his head under the leaves.

Then came the whooshing of wings.

Big wings.

Bloody big wings.

'Shit,' he said again, with more feeling.

From the sound of it the dragon was circling the quarry, checking out the situation. As it passed overhead Travis thought he could feel the pressure of a downdraft on his thin layer of leaves. *This mother is sodding enormous*, he told himself worriedly. The .45 automatic felt like it was a feather in his grip. What he needed was a rocket launcher.

The flapping of the wings grew louder. The dragon was coming in to land. *Thump*. The ground shook. It was down.

Very slowly he raised his head and peered out through the leaves.

And saw Garaptor. It was a big dragon indeed, about fifty feet from head to tail. And also a very ugly one. Its grey, sagging skin was covered with wart-like growths and its head would have got a sympathy vote from a gargoyle.

It had landed right in front of Princess Beatrice and was staring down at her with a hungry glint in the one blood-shot eye that Travis could see from his position. The Princess, he noted, was doing a pretty good job of looking defiant, which couldn't have been easy under the circumstances. The head began to lower itself towards her. *Time to move*, he thought, and began to rise up from his hiding place.

He froze.

Something was happening to the dragon. Something weird. Its outline had become all fuzzy and indistinct, as if he was peering at it through out-of-focus glasses. And then it began to . . . *shrink* . . .

It kept shrinking until it had become the size of a man on all fours. Then the form became sharply focussed and Travis saw that it *was* a man on all fours. A naked old man with long, dirty white hair. And when he stood Travis realized that he was a dirty old man in more than one sense of the word. He was sporting a sizeable erection.

The Princess gave a shocked gasp. Then exclaimed, '*You!*'

The old man cackled an old man's dirty cackle. 'Never thought you'd see me again, did you, Princess Beatrice? Eh? Oh, I've waited such a long time for this moment.' He slowly reached out a dirty, clawed hand towards the bodice of her gown. And he actually started to drool as he did so.

Travis decided it was time to act.

Chapter Four

Travis leapt up. 'Okay, that's near enough!' he yelled, pointing the Colt at the naked old man who turned and stared at him in surprise. The Princess looked equally surprised.

'What trickery is this?!' cried the old man. He turned back to the Princess. 'Who is this champion of yours, skulking in the bushes like a common thief?'

'I've never seen him before,' she replied. 'And *you* can't talk, Moonglot! Pretending to be a dragon . . .'

Travis walked towards them, keeping the gun pointing at the old man. He was confused. *Now what?* he wondered. Shooting a dragon was one thing but shooting an unarmed, naked old man was something else.

The old man, seemingly recovered from his initial surprise, regarded Travis calmly. 'Who are you?' he asked.

'I'm Travis Thomson, freelance adventurer and journalist.'

'Journalist?' repeated the old man, with a frown. 'Is that some sort of magician?'

'Well, I suppose I could be described as a magician with words . . .'

The old man gave the pistol a look and said, 'And that thing in your hand; is it a weapon or a talisman?'

Travis came to a halt about six feet from him. 'Kind of both,' he said, 'so please don't do anything that will force me to use it.'

The old man looked at the Colt .45 again. 'It appears to be a feeble little thing. It even has a hole in its end.'

'That hole spews out death,' said Travis, trying for a *gravitas* of tone he didn't think he was quite achieving.

'Kill him now!' cried the Princess to Travis. 'He's a sorcerer and an evil one! Don't give him the chance to . . .'

'Shut up, your Highness!' the old man snapped at her. 'I will be back to enjoy your sweet flesh just as soon as I deal with this fool.' He made a gesture with his hands and muttered something under his breath. Then Travis saw that the old man's form was beginning to go out of focus.

Travis fired three shots at the wavering shape, fearing that he had left it too late and was about to find himself facing one very large, pissed-off dragon. But the old man came back into focus again. He was tottering from side to side and he now had three ragged holes in his thin chest. Blood began to trickle from them. The old man looked down at the perforations with a bemused expression, then looked again at the .45. 'I'm impressed,' he wheezed then fell backwards and lay still. Travis thought the show was over but then black smoke began to pour from the body's various orifices. As the smoke formed a cloud above, the corpse itself began to shrivel. Soon there was nothing remaining of it but dust. The black cloud began to blow away in the light breeze.

Travis looked at Princess Beatrice. 'Is that it?' he asked.

'Yes. He's dead. Thank the Green Queen. And thank you too, sir.'

'All part of the service.' He moved closer to her, feeling her beauty on his face like the warmth from a fire. Whoever designed the software that had created her was clearly touched by genius. Hard to believe it could have been Prenderghast. No. He preferred to believe, for the moment, that she was actually genuine flesh and blood. He smiled at her and said, 'I gather you knew our late dragon and sorcerer.'

'Yes. His name was Moonglot. He used to be the Court Sorcerer until he was caught doing disgusting things to small children. My father banished him but he swore he would get revenge on both king and the kingdom.' She held out her manacled arms. 'Can you do anything about these?'

He inspected the heavy chain. 'I hope so,' he told her. He took hold of the length of chain between her wrists and put the muzzle of the gun close to it, pointing downwards. 'Turn your head away,' he warned her, 'I'm not sure what's going to happen. . .' Which was true. Closing his eyes and hoping for the best, he pulled the trigger. The automatic jarred his arm and something whizzed past his right ear. He opened his eyes. Several links of the chain had shattered, the metal old and brittle. He pulled the rest of the chain through the iron rings on the post and shackles and the Princess was free. She still had the cuffs on her wrists but they could be easily removed back in Vallium.

'I thank you again, sir,' she said, taking a deep breath. 'That is a very powerful talisman you have there.'

'I know,' he said as he holstered the automatic. Then he gave a cry of pain as something sharp dug into the calf of his right leg. He looked down. It was that damned goblin. Obviously annoyed at being thwarted from his expectations concerning the left-overs he had stuck his fork into Travis's leg. Travis aimed a kick at him but the goblin was already scuttling away with his cutlery. He disappeared among the rocks.

'Are you alright?' the Princess asked him.

'Yeah. Just a little prick. And the wound is nothing much either,' he said, rubbing his injured leg. 'Well, let's get going. My horse isn't far from here.'

'To where?'

'Back to your kingdom, of course.'

She shook her head. 'No.'

'What do you mean *no*? It's all planned. I take you back to your father, he showers me with gold and maybe a few bags stuffed with an assortment of precious stones and I'm on my way.'

She shook her head again and folded her arms defiantly across her bosom. 'I'm not going back there.'

'You must do! It's your home!'

'You've been to Vallium, haven't you?'

'Well, yeah. Briefly.'

'Then would you go back there, willingly?'

He thought about it. 'No, I guess not, but you're its Princess. You belong there. And there's your father . . .'

'That rat? I hate him. He drove my mother to suicide. She threw herself from the south tower three years ago.'

'Hey, I'm sorry, but you have to go back. Where else can you go?'

'I can go wherever you're going. For a time at least.'

It was his turn to shake his head. 'Out of the question. And, no offence, your Highness, but I need the money.'

'I don't want to go back,' she said firmly. 'And, if you force me to, I'll tell my father you raped me. You can imagine, I'm sure, what my father would do to you if I told him that.'

Travis spent a few moments thinking about hot lead. 'But your Highness, I saved your life! You wouldn't do that to me!'

'I'm sorry, I don't want to, but I'm desperate. I'm not going back to him.'

His thoughts raced. Round in circles. Uselessly. 'But . . . but . . .' he said, desperately. 'Well, for a start I have no money. How could we live?'

She glanced down at her hands. 'My father stripped all my rings from me before we left the castle. I have nothing of value we could sell.'

Travis thought there was room for debate on that point but decided not to pursue the subject. 'See then? How could we survive?'

'What about you? Don't you have anything at all? she asked him.

'Only my horse, and I need him.' And as he spoke he heard the sound of approaching hooves. Could it be that good ol' Whiplash was turning up right on cue like Trigger the Wonder Horse? He turned and looked. No, of course not. It was one of the knights riding towards them. Travis slowly drew his gun.

The knight rode up to them, brought his steed to a halt and raised his visor.

'Sir Rodney!' exclaimed the Princess. 'You astound me!'

'My darling, I had to disobey your father and return to you! I swore to myself that if I couldn't rescue you I would die with you!' He looked around. 'But where is the dragon?' And then he pointed his lance at Travis. 'And who is this fop?'

'He calls himself Travis. And, despite his foppish appearance, he saved my life. He killed Garaptor.'

'He did?' said Sir Rodney, not sounding even slightly convinced. He looked around again. 'How did the fop manage that? And where's the carcass?'

'He has a magic talisman. Show him, Travis.'

Feeling irritated by being called a fop three times in as many sentences, Travis held up the automatic. Sir Rodney gave it a puzzled glance. 'You killed a dragon with *that*?'

'He did indeed,' said the Princess. 'As for the corpse, it disappeared in a puff of smoke.'

Sir Rodney stared at her. 'Oh really?'

'It's a bit difficult to explain,' she told him, 'But Garaptor wasn't a real dragon. It was Moonglot, my father's old sorcerer. He must have become considerably more powerful over the years because he'd acquired the ability to change himself into a dragon. He certainly couldn't do that when he was at my father's court, though at one of my birthday parties he did turn himself into a vole.' She paused. 'You do remember Moonglot, don't you?'

'Uh, no, I don't believe I do, your Highness,' said Sir Rodney. 'Sorry,' he added.

'I suppose he was banished before you joined the court. Anyway, after arriving as a dragon he turned himself back into Moonglot with the obvious intention of ravishing me. No doubt when he had satisfied his vile lusts he would have turned himself back into Garaptor and devoured me. I fear he must have done the same with all the sacrificial virgins.' She shook her head with disgust. 'Horrible man. Fortunately Travis killed him before he could change himself back into a dragon. And then his body just sort of turned into smoke and blew away.'

Sir Rodney sat there silently for a while, then he said, 'Er, yes. Of course. All makes perfect sense.' He dismounted, with difficulty, leant his lance against the side of his horse and extended his hand to the Princess. 'But whatever happened here the important thing is that you're safe. Now allow me to assist you onto my steed and we shall return to Vallium. Your father will be delighted to see you alive and unharmed.'

She ignored his outstretched hand. 'No, Rodney, I'm not coming back with you.'

He looked at her blankly. 'Pardon?'

'You heard me. I'm not returning to Vallium. I'm running away with Travis here. He's an adventurer. *And* a journalist, whatever that is. I want to be like him. I want to see the world. I want to travel and have adventures.'

'Er, it's not quite like that . . .' Travis tried to tell her, but she wasn't listening.

Sir Rodney was now looking at her with a horrified expression. 'But, your Highness, you can't do that! You're a Princess! It's out of the question!'

'Well, that's what I'm *going* to do. My mind's made up.'

Sir Rodney then began looking hard at Travis. 'I think I see now what has happened. . .' He pointed at Travis. '*He* is the wicked sorcerer! He has befuddled your mind with his magic!'

'Oh, rubbish, Rodney,' she said.

But Sir Rodney had found an explanation that suited him perfectly and he clearly intended to hang on to it. He began to draw his sword.

Travis backed away. 'Hey, none of this running off together stuff was my idea,' he protested to him, 'it's all her's! I wanted to take her back to her father and claim a bloody big reward . . .'

'Bloody big', he saw, could also be applied to Sir Rodney's sword. The knight advanced on Travis. Travis backed away even faster.

'Use your talisman on him, Travis,' called the Princess. 'But don't kill him. Just knock the stuffing out of him.'

'I'm sorry, your Highness,' he called back, 'but this thing doesn't have a fine tuner.'

Sir Rodney made a rush at him, though as rushes go it was a slow one because of his heavy and awkwardly constructed armour. Travis easily side-stepped out of danger. 'Please, Sir Rodney, I don't want to hurt you!'

'Huh-ha!' guffawed Sir Rodney as he made another slow and clumsy charge at Travis. 'You may have befuddled the

Princess's weak womanly mind with your trickery but you're dealing with a man and a knight of the realm now! Prepare to die!' With his sword held high he made another charge at Travis.

Sod this for a game of soldiers, thought Travis and aimed the gun low at Sir Rodney's feet. He fired. Sir Rodney fell with a cry of pain and a crash of metal. Fearing that he had seriously injured him, Travis walked over to the moaning knight. 'Sorry, but I warned you,' he said as he leaned over him and examined his armour. To his relief he found the bullet hole was on the end of Sir Rodney's armoured right boot.

The Princess hurried over. 'I told you not to kill him,' she said, disapprovingly.

'He's not going to die . . .' *Unless it's from shock*, Travis thought bleakly. '. . . But he may have lost a couple of toes.'

'*Owwww! Arghhhh! Ooooarghhh!*' cried Sir Rodney. He tried again to sit up and failed once more. Travis, with an effort, heaved him into a sitting position. As the Princess knelt beside Rodney and removed his helmet, Travis went about the confusing task of undoing and removing his right boot. The latter activity produced even louder cries of pain.

'Oh, be quiet, you big baby!' admonished the Princess. Travis succeeded in getting the leather and metal boot off Rodney's foot, revealing a dirty brown sock sodden with blood around the toe area. He pulled the sock off and examined the damage. He felt nauseous. Rodney's big toe was missing. Presumably it was still in the sock. Travis didn't feel inclined to look for it. Fortunately the wound wasn't bleeding too much.

'He should be alright,' he told the Princess, who was tearing a strip from the hem of her sacrificial dress to make a bandage. 'But he'll need help to get back to Vallium.' He was hoping that she might have changed her mind about running away. But no. She said, as she bandaged Rodney's foot, 'There'll be a patrol arriving here later, to confirm that the dragon has devoured me. They'll take him back.'

'Oh,' said Travis. 'But that still leaves us with the problem of money.'

'Not any more,' she said brightly. She tapped Sir Rodney's breastplate. 'Most likely Rodney's purse will be somewhere under all that. And the armour itself is valuable. We can take it and sell it along the way. And his weapon too . . . His horse I'll need for myself.'

Rodney yelped again but not from the pain. 'Princess! I can't believe what I'm hearing! Truly this wicked magician has laid claim to your senses!'

She began undoing the buckles of his armour. 'The only one who has laid claim to my senses is *me*. I should have done it long ago. Weak, womanly mind, eh? I won't forget that. And stop fretting. My father will surely reimburse you . . . if he doesn't have you executed for disobeying his orders.'

Rodney tried to struggle. She cuffed him over the head. 'Stop that or I'll have Travis use his talisman on you again.' Rodney went very still. But he said, in a quiet voice, 'I can't believe you're doing this to me, your Highness. After all we've meant to each other.'

'Oh, spare me your romantic nonsense, Rodney. All I ever saw in you was the hopeful means of losing my virginity, but you let me down, you pompous clown.'

Rodney glared at Travis. 'This is all *your* fault, magician!' he snarled. 'You have beguiled my darling Princess Beatrice. And for that you must die! I vow I will never rest until I have claimed vengeance!'

'Oh dear, I'm sure you've got Travis shaking in his boots,' said the Princess with a laugh. 'Isn't that so, Travis?'

Travis didn't answer.

About ten minutes later they were ready to go. Sir Rodney was sitting on the ground clad only in what passed for underpants on Samella. He was securely trussed up with strips of cloth made from the Princess's sacrificial gown. One of the strips was around his mouth, keeping him mercifully quiet. The sacrificial gown had become radically mini by the time she'd finished and Travis had felt both disappointed and relieved when she'd gone behind a bush to change into Rodney's clothes.

She was now toying with her long, black hair. 'Travis, if I wore your hat with my hair all pushed up under it, do you think I could pass for a boy?'

'No,' he said, truthfully.

But she held out her hand for his hat anyway. Dutifully, he gave it to her. She put it on and tucked her hair up under it. 'How do I look?' she asked him when she was finished. He inspected her. Despite the man's clothes and the concealed hair she still looked like a stunningly beautiful young woman. But he said, 'It's amazing the difference it makes . . . Andy.'

She laughed. 'Andy? What kind of name is that?'

'It's short for Andrew.'

'Andrew,' she repeated slowly. 'Yes, I like that. Yes, from now on I shall be known as Andrew. And I'll pretend to be your young manservant.' She went and patted Sir Rodney on the head. 'Goodbye, Rodney, you silly man. And when you see my father tell him I think he's an absolute pig. Also warn him that if he sends anyone to try and take me back they will be certain to fall victim to my protector's powerful talisman.'

Rodney made angry but muffled sounds from behind the gag. She smiled at him and walked over to his horse, which had his armour, lance, shield and sword strapped to its side. To Travis she said, 'Help me mount and we'll be on our way.'

He stood beside the horse, leaned forward and formed a support with his hands clamped together. She raised a dainty bare foot – acquiring a pair of boots for her was going to be one of their first priorities – and placed it in his hands. Then, gripping one of his shoulders, she raised herself onto the saddle. 'Good. Now lead the way to where you have hidden your own steed.'

'Yes, your Highness,' he said as he took hold of the bridle.

'Oh, don't call me that! If our masquerade is to succeed you must become used to calling me Andrew . . . or Andy.'

Their 'masquerade' had as much chance of success as an English tennis player but he decided it would be simpler to humour her. 'Alright, *Andy*,' he said as he began leading the horse towards the entrance of the quarry. 'But to ensure full authenticity I think you're going to need some lessons on how to behave as a servant.'

'Yes, you're right,' she said, nodding.

'And there's one other subject I must raise with you,' he told her.

'What's that?'

'His name's Jack.'

Chapter Five

'Is this kind of like *Groundhog Day*?' Travis had asked Jack.

'Is it like what?' Jack had asked.

This conversation had taken place in the third week after Travis's arrival. They had made camp in a clearing out of sight of the road they were travelling along. Earlier that morning they'd had an unpleasant encounter with a group of bandits. Travis had been obliged to shoot one of them dead before the others had given up their attempt to overpower them and fled. Back then Travis had had no qualms about shooting anybody, still believing, in the main, that this was a computerized, make-believe world.

'*Groundhog Day*. The movie starring Bill Murray.'

Jack shook his head. 'It must have come out after Prenderghast zapped me.'

'When was that?'

'August, 1992. It was a Wednesday.'

'Yes, you would have missed it. Bill Murray plays this cynical TV guy stuck in a small, hick town. He's also got stuck in the same day. He has to live the same day over and over again. It's not exactly the same for him – he can influence events each time – but at the end of the day he wakes up at the start of the same day again . . .'

Jack suddenly flew into the air and made a grab at a passing small bird. He missed and, muttering a curse, settled back on the ground. 'Cut to the chase,' he told Travis.

'Well, after the Murray character adjusts to the realization that he's stuck in the one day indefinitely he tries to use the situation to seduce his co-worker, who is played by Andie MacDowell . . . You know of her don't you?'

'Sure. *Sex, Lies and Videotape* and other stuff. Good looking babe. Now *Sex* . . . that was a clever little job. Made on a shoestring but grossed a goddamn fortune. And not even one good tit shot either. Now, if I'd made it I would have . . .'

'Hey, I'm trying to make a point here.'

'Jeez . . .' muttered Jack and produced his magic pack of Marlboro.

'So Murray uses all these devious schemes to get MacDowell into bed, but they don't work. In the meantime, of course, he falls in love with her. The point is that only when Murray uses his unique position to *help* other people in the town, when he starts acting unselfishly, does he win MacDowell's love. And once that happens he is freed from the curse of being trapped in that single day. And free to live happily ever after with MacDowell.'

'This movie make money?' asked Jack.

'Yes. It was a box office hit.'

'Jeez. So what's your angle?'

'Well, am I being taught a lesson, like the Bill Murray character? Do I have to somehow improve myself before I'm allowed to return to the real world?'

Jack cackled wildly. Then he said, 'You serious? You think you're here on some moral improvement course? Hah!'

'I thought it might be a possible explanation,' said Travis.

'Listen dickwit,' said Jack, stabbing his cigarette in Travis's direction, 'Prenderghast doesn't give a shit about your moral welfare. You're here because you made him mad at you. Like I did. You're not here to meet some babe and fall in love. You're here to have a bad time. And you're going to be stuck here until you find the friggin Key, like I told you before.'

Travis sighed deeply. 'The Key. Yes, I know you keep telling me I have to find the Key but you won't tell me how, or even what it looks like.'

'That's because I don't know myself, dickwit.' He flipped the extinguished butt of the cigarette away from him.

Travis was silent for a time. It was starting to get cool as the sun sank towards the horizon. He pulled his cape tighter around him and wished they could risk lighting a fire but there were likely to be more bandits in the vicinity. 'And how do you get out of here? Are you looking for a Key of your own?' he finally asked Jack.

'No. There's no Key for me. I'm here for the duration. I'm here until you either find your Key or get yourself killed?'

'Let's look on the bright side and presume I succeed in finding this Key before I get killed. Where do you go then?'

'Dunno. I only hope it's not back to the place where I was before this.'

'And where was that?'

The demon shuddered. 'Don't ask.'

Travis didn't. But he did ask, 'What exactly did you do to Prenderghast to make him so mad at you?'

'I cheated him. Or I tried to. If only I knew then what I found out later about him . . .' He shuddered again.

'So how did you cheat him?'

'He came to me and said he wanted to set up a deal making a series of low-budget exploitation movies. But he wanted them made on special equipment with special film stock that he would provide. I just thought he was some eccentric old fool with more bucks than sense. So I took his money and went on a vacation. I was having a high old time in Vegas when he found me. He made it very clear that I hadn't been dealing with an eccentric old fool, but by then it was too late for apologies.' He took out another cigarette and lit it.

Travis stared at the demon. He made it all sound so *real*. Travis looked around the clearing, at the darkening woods beyond. Perhaps, as incredible as it might seem, he really was on another world on an entirely different plane of existence, whatever that was. And Prenderghast wasn't just some egomaniacal millionaire toy manufacturer but an alien entity with almost limitless powers . . . a god-like being who had a serious grudge against him.

He was distracted from this grim and morbid line of thought when two fairies, their wings brightly incandescent with reds, greens and yellows, suddenly flew into the clearing and began to chase each other about. But their game was rudely halted when Jack spat drops of molten hot saliva at them. They fled, making high-pitched sounds of annoyance as they went.

'Can't stand bloody fairies,' muttered Jack.

No, thought Travis, *this whole thing is impossible. None of it is real.*

I hope.

Whiplash and Jack were where he had left them, concealed in a dense thicket. Jack, predictably, made a long wolf-whistle when he saw Beatrice. 'Wow, that's some babe!' he said, approvingly. 'The Princess herself, I presume.' He fluttered up from Whiplash's saddle and landed on the head of her borrowed steed. He leered at her. She flinched away from him, looking disgusted. 'But I didn't realize she was a cross-dresser,' the demon continued.

'She's in disguise,' explained Travis.

'Oh, *sure* she is. And I'm Sharon Stone. But I sure approve. How kinky can you get?' He smacked his lips suggestively.

'Yuck,' said Beatrice. 'He's even more revolting than you warned, Travis. And he smells awful!'

Jack leaned closer to her. 'But you babe, on the contrary, smell just great.' He turned and grinned at Travis. 'I'm impressed. I didn't really think you had a chance in hell. So how did you manage to kill the virgin muncher?'

'It was only a part-time dragon. It was actually a sorcerer pretending to be a dragon. I got him when he was in human form.'

'Good for you, dickwit. So all we have to do now is go back to Vallium and pick up the loot from her father.'

Travis shook his head. 'We have a slight complication.'

'What kind of slight complication?' asked Jack, suspiciously.

Travis pointed at the Princess and told Jack about her determination not to return to Vallium and her father. 'She wants to come with us – well, with *me* – and have adventures and stuff.'

Jack said, 'She's nuts.' Then he turned to her and said,

'You're nuts, babe. We live rough, babe, really rough. A few days and nights and you'll be wishing you were back in your nice, comfortable castle.'

'No. I won't,' she said firmly, 'and the castle is anything but comfortable, anyway.'

'Look, no offence, babe, but we need the money that returning your beautiful, uneaten hide back to your father would get us. We're broke.'

'Not exactly,' said Travis as he held up Sir Rodney's purse. 'And we have that armour to sell as well.'

Jack looked at the armour and the weapons strapped to it. 'Where did all that come from?'

Travis told him about the unfortunate Sir Rodney. Jack laughed.

'And speaking of Sir Rodney,' said Beatrice, 'when he arrives back in Vallium he's sure to accuse you of abducting me. And then my father, with his precious honour to think of, will send soldiers after us. We should start travelling right away.'

'And maybe, babe,' said Jack, 'we should just take you back to Vallium anyway, no matter what you want.'

'Er, that's out of the question, Jack,' Travis said, explaining about Beatrice's threat and the inevitable hot lead treatment that would follow.

'Ouch,' said Jack, wincing. 'Well, I see your point.'

'Yeah,' said Travis and mounted Whiplash. 'And she's right about making tracks out of here. Fast.'

'Before we go,' said Beatrice, 'is there any way of getting these off me? They're not only uncomfortable but they're going to arouse suspicion.' She held up her manacled wrists.

'No problem, babe. Let me see those.' Jack reached towards her hands. She initially flinched away from him again but then held out her hands to him. He gripped one of the manacles with his long, thin fingers and pulled. The manacle came apart with a snapping sound. He did the same with the other one. He winked at Beatrice and said, 'I'm pretty strong for such a little guy, and I'm well-endowed in other areas as well . . .'

'That's enough, Jack. Get back here.'

The demon reluctantly rose in the air and fluttered back to his usual perch on Whiplash's head. 'Just having some fun,' he said sourly.

'Well, behave yourself. She's a Princess. But don't call her that. She intends to pass herself off as my young manservant.'

'The way she looks? You've got to be kidding!'

'I know, but humour her, will you?'

'Oh sure. So what do I call her?'

'Andy.'

'Andy? *Andy?*' And then Jack cackled wildly.

'Let's go,' said Travis, irritably.

Keeping to the back trails and as far away from the so-called 'main roads' as possible, they moved as fast as they could, though that wasn't very fast since Beatrice's borrowed steed kept slowing down. 'It'll be better once we get rid of all that armour and stuff,' Travis told Beatrice, when once again the horse's canter became a tired walk.

'We can sell it at the first town we come to, can't we?' she asked.

'Probably wise to avoid any towns for the time being. If we sell the armour too soon it'll be a dead giveaway of which direction we're travelling in when your father's men hear of it.'

'I wish we could just dump it. Hide it in the woods.'

'So do I but the money in Sir Rodney's purse won't last us very long. We need the sovereigns that selling the armour and weapons will bring us.'

'I suppose so,' she sighed. Then, some moments later, she asked. 'Why do you travel with that horrible demon?'

'Believe me, it's not by choice,' he said, with feeling. He looked up into the sky. Thankfully, Jack had gone off on a scouting mission and there was no sign of his imminent return. 'We're tied together by a sort of contractual agreement we can't break – for the time being.'

'I don't understand,' she said.

'Neither do I, to be honest. It's all very confusing.'

She mulled this over for a time, then asked, 'What land do you come from? It's clear from the manner in which you speak that you are a foreigner.'

'I am very much a foreigner.' Then he laughed and said, 'I come from a galaxy far, far away.'

'A what?'

'I come from another world, Beatrice. Or so I've been told.'

'Oh,' she said, with understanding. 'You mean you come from Avedon,' she said and pointed up towards Samella's largest moon, which Travis knew was inhabited.

'No, not Avedon. My world is much, much further away.'

'Really?' She sounded suspicious now. 'I know of no such world. How did you get here?'

'That I don't know. Magic, it seems.'

'Oh,' she said, as if that explained everything. 'And what is your world like?'

'Very different from this one.'

'In what way?'

'That would take a long time to describe.'

'Is it better than Samella?'

'For a few people – the lucky ones who live in the richer countries. But for most of my world's population, life's a bitch. Just like here.'

'Did you come from one of the richer countries?'

'Well, it *used* to be rich but the government's been doing its best to change all that.'

'Do you miss it?'

'Sure. And my family and friends, naturally, and my girlfriend, Heather. I miss things like newspapers, radio and television, restaurants, cinemas, good wine, my car . . . but most of all I miss indoor plumbing and toilet paper.'

'Most of what you said means nothing to me.'

'I know . . . sorry.'

'What, for example is your girlfriend? A girl who happens to be your friend? Any why do you only have one woman friend? Is it a law in your world?'

Travis laughed. 'No, it's not a law. A girlfriend is . . . a female friend who is *more* than just a friend.'

She mused on this for a while and then said, 'Oh, you mean she's your lover?'

'Yes, that's right,' he said, glancing at her. He looked at her a lot. And every time he did, her beauty made his blood tingle.

'So you'll be marrying her when you return to your own world?' she asked.

Travis hesitated. He'd really never seen Heather and he getting married. 'I don't think so,' he said finally.

'You don't love her?'

'I don't know,' he answered honestly. 'Sometimes I think I do, but at other times I'm not sure. I like her a lot. She's great company.'

'And she's a good lover?'

He glanced at her again. Her expression was serious. 'Yes, she is,' he told her, *but then she's had a lot of practice*, he added to himself.

Beatrice sighed. 'I've never made love to anyone.'

'Being a virgin, I guess that comes with the territory.'

'I know all about it, of course. Both my ladies-in-waiting have lovers and I have made them tell me all the details. It sounds wonderful.'

'Well, a lot of the time it is. Except when you've had one bottle of wine too many.' The thought of the beautiful Beatrice in a love-making situation was beginning to cause Travis some discomfort in the vicinity of his cod-piece. He decided it would be best to change the subject. 'Are you sure you're going to be able to give up your former life of luxury so easily? Jack wasn't exaggerating when he told you how rough we often have it on the road. And he didn't even mention the goats' testicle stew.'

'I'm not some soft, helpless little girl,' she said firmly, 'I've been riding to the hunt since I was a girl. I'm an expert on a horse and I'm a fine shot with a bow and arrow.'

'Still, it's going to be a huge wrench for you,' he said. 'You might change your mind eventually.'

'No, I won't.'

He shrugged. 'If you say so. But what about your long-term future?'

'Look, it's a big world and I've seen a small corner of it. And perhaps I may even come and visit your world as well when you decide to return to it.'

Taken by surprise, he didn't know how to answer her.

'Great idea, babe,' said a voice from overhead. Jack had returned. 'And if you play your cards right with me I'll get you into the movies. You'll be a star, babe, believe me.'

Chapter Six

'Andy? *Andy!* Jeez, you kill me, dickwit,' Jack sneered.

'Given half a chance,' muttered Travis.

'You really thinking she's your Key? Your way out of this mess like in that movie you were telling me about?' Jack sniggered. 'No way, *José*.'

'The name just sprang to mind, that's all,' said Travis, defensively. 'I know she doesn't look like Andie MacDowell. But how do you know she isn't the Key? You've said yourself you have no idea what it is. It *could* be a person.'

'Yeah, but I do know a bit about how Prenderghast thinks and having that babe as your exit visa isn't his style.'

'You're probably right,' sighed Travis, poking the embers of the fire with the tip of his sword. They had made camp beside a small stream. Travis hoped the roadside vendor they'd bought some food from that afternoon had been right about this not being bandit country, since they'd felt it was safe to light a fire.

After they'd finished eating Beatrice had excused herself and went downstream to do whatever it was she was still doing. Attending to her toiletries, he presumed. He wondered how she was making out in the toilet paper department. But then he guessed they didn't have toilet paper in her castle either. What did the aristocrats use instead? Perfumed handkerchiefs? He remembered that the ancient Romans used to use little sponges on the end of sticks . . .

He would have to get over this obsession with toilet paper. It was starting to get unhealthy. But everything on this world seemed to be unhealthy.

Then again, that wasn't really true. Some common Earth diseases didn't seem to exist on Samella. Sexual diseases, for example, seemed to be entirely absent – thank goodness.

And leprosy. He hadn't seen any cases of leprosy during his travels. But people here certainly suffered from things like colds and influenza, and at an inn once he saw an old man who was clearly dying of pneumonia. He stared up at the moons and stars and wondered, not for the first time, just how much the laws of physics here had in common with those of his own universe. There had to be some similarities. Like gravity. It must work the same way here. He picked up a stone and dropped it. Yes, it seemed to fall at exactly the same rate as one would on Earth. So gravity was just as mystifying a process to him here as it was back on his own world. The big difference was that in this universe magic worked. And *how*. But at least Samella wasn't flat, shaped like an upturned dinner plate and sitting on the back of some bloody great elephant turtle.

'The babe doth returneth,' said Jack.

Travis looked and saw Beatrice coming back up the side of the stream. She had her arms wrapped around her. 'It's getting cold,' she said as she approached them.

'See? I knew it,' sneered Jack. 'Complaining already.'

'I'm not complaining,' she said as she sat down next to Travis. 'I'm pointing out a simple fact.'

'Jack, go find some more wood for the fire,' Travis ordered.

'Go hump yourself,' replied Jack, giving him the finger.

Travis groaned and started to rise. He knew there'd been no chance that the demon would obey him. But then he froze when Jack suddenly said, 'I hear voices! Coming this way.'

Travis listened hard. Yes, Jack was right. High-pitched but male voices. Three of them, he figured. He reached for the automatic in his holster. Beatrice, he noted, had already drawn the dagger she'd appropriated from Sir Rodney. She too slowly stood up.

They waited.

The voices drew nearer. Then, out of the trees, three figures emerged. When they saw Travis and the others they came to an abrupt halt and their chatter instantly dried up. Both groups stared at each other. Travis saw three slim male figures with pointed ears and blond hair, dressed in tight-fitting tunics which seemed to be made of different coloured leaves. Then the silence was broken by Jack saying loudly, 'Oh no, that's all we need! A bunch of bloody elves!'

One of the elves put his hand on his hip and said haughtily, 'Oooh, girls, listen to Miss Bat Features!'

Jack rose into the air and angrily spat fiery saliva at the elf who had spoken. But the elf, grinning, merely raised his hand and the molten spit disappeared in a flash of golden light. At the same moment a golden net appeared above Jack. It fell on him, fouled his wings and he crashed to the ground. Spluttering a string of obscenities he struggled in vain to free himself from the glowing net.

Travis stared at the struggling demon and then back at the three grinning elves. The thought of Jack helpless had its attraction, but his sense of justice *just* won out. 'Let him go,' he said, his hand still resting on the butt of the gun.

'Give us one good reason, sugarbuns,' said another of the elves as they began to advance on Travis and Beatrice. Travis wasn't sure what to do. Just how big a threat did they present? They looked harmless enough, but there was more than a hint of gleeful malice in their large, golden, almond-shaped eyes. He decided to wait and see what developed, leaving the gun in its holster.

The three elves encircled Beatrice and him, looking them slowly up and down with lascivious smiles. Beatrice quickly drew the bulk of their attention. 'Well, well, you're a very pretty boy,' said one of them to Beatrice, giving her an appreciative pat on her bottom. 'A juicy plum indeed. And one I would dearly love to sink my teeth into . . .'

'Get away from me!' hissed Beatrice, waving her dagger in a threatening manner. The elf laughed, made a gesture with the same hand that had just patted her, and the dagger, suddenly surrounded by a golden glow, then turned into a red rose on a long stem. 'For you, gorgeous one,' said the elf and made a bow as he offered it to her. 'Now how would you like to go for a little walk in the woods with me?'

'Boy, are you barking up the wrong tree, acorn head!' Jack laughed scornfully from inside his net.

'What my companion is trying to tell you is that this pretty "boy" is really a pretty girl,' said Travis, surprised that Beatrice's unlikely disguise had actually fooled the elves for even a moment. But perhaps sheer wishful thinking had blinded them to the obvious.

'Nonsense,' said her chief admirer, but he tentatively prodded her in the chest just the same. Travis knew she had bound up her breasts with strips of cloth but there was no concealing their existence beneath her jacket. The elf withdrew his hand as if stung. 'Oh, dragon farts! They're speaking the truth! It's female!'

'Those are the breaks,' said Travis.

The three elves turned all their attention to him. 'So that just leaves you to provide us with some sport, sugarbuns,' said one of them without enthusiasm. The elf grabbed Travis's cod-piece and squeezed. Then he sighed and said, 'I suppose beggars can't be choosers.'

Travis had had enough. He drew the gun and levelled it at them. 'Okay, back off, you bunch of raving fairies!'

'We're not fairies, we're *elves*,' said one haughtily. Another of them, staring at the automatic with disdain, said, 'If that's your weapon, darling, it's awfully small.'

'It's a Colt .45 automatic!' called Jack. 'It's the most powerful handgun in the world – hell, it's the *only* frigging handgun in the world – and it'll blow your fruity heads clean off!'

'Just what is that prune-faced old queen ranting about?' asked one of them.

'He's talking about this,' said Travis hefting the gun. 'It's a powerful weapon. Very dangerous indeed. So I'd advise you to get going.'

'He's speaking the truth,' said Beatrice. 'It's a very powerful talisman. I've seen him use it.'

The elves glanced at each other and then one of them raised a limp hand. 'I suppose we'd better be on the safe side, girls,' he said. A golden glow surrounded the gun. Travis stared at it in apprehension, fearing he was suddenly going to find himself holding a bunch of daisies.

But the automatic pistol resolutely remained an automatic pistol. The three elves glanced at each other again, this time nervously. 'What kind of magic is this?' asked one.

'Hah!' cried Jack triumphantly. 'That's given you mincing ninnies a jolt in the balls, hasn't it?' Then to Travis he called, 'Give 'em a demonstration, Travis. Shoot at a tree. And if that doesn't work, shoot one of them!'

Travis obliged.He picked out a nearby tree, aimed the gun at it and fired. The elves jumped as the weapon made a satisfactorily loud sound and spat flame. Just as satisfactory was the large crater that appeared in the tree trunk. Chips of wood flew through the air and there was the familiar acrid smell of gunpowder. The elves turned and stared at the gun, their expressions puzzled and wary. Travis pointed it at them each in turn. They all flinched. 'Well, girls,' said one of them finally, 'it looks like sugarbuns here has more in his cod-piece than we thought. I suggest we leave these lovely people to their own devices and continue our stroll . . .' They began to back away. Jack cried, 'Hey, what about me?! Let me out of this thing, you fruitcakes!'

Travis was tempted to leave Jack in the net for the time being but knew he'd have to release him sooner or later, and if it was later the demon would be in an even fouler mood. 'Do as he says,' he told the elves. One of them raised a hand and gestured. The net vanished in a cloud of golden dust. Jack stood up, shaking himself and stretching his wings. 'About time, you bunch of mattress-munching, cod-piece sniffing, fruitheads!' he snarled. 'Now get out of here before I tell my friend to fill you full of holes!'

'Elvophobe,' accused one of the elves. Then they turned, joined hands and disappeared into the trees. *Phew*, thought Travis. Once he was satisfied they were really gone he holstered the gun and went over to Beatrice. 'You alright?'

Before she could say anything Jack flew into the air and exploded, metaphorically speaking. 'Of course *she's* alright! I was the one who nearly got strangled to death in that goddamn net! Why don't you ask me if *I'm* alright, dickwit?!' He began to orbit Travis's head at a perilously close range.

'Because you're obviously fine,' said Travis, trying to brush him away as one would to an annoying fly. 'We all seem to be just fine. Now let's get some rest before we're visited by a group of sex-crazed succubi or a bunch of pixilated pixies . . .'

But Jack kept flying round his head. 'I knew this babe was going to be trouble from the moment I saw her. You're falling for her, aren't you?'

'Don't be ridiculous, Jack!' Travis protested. 'Anyway, how can I fall for her when I know that, basically, she isn't even *real*!?'

'Because you're a *dickwit*, dickwit!'

'What did you say?' asked Beatrice. 'What do you mean, I'm not real?'

Travis, belatedly, realized he'd put his foot in it. 'Oh, nothing. Pay no attention to what I said, please, Beatrice.'

'No, please explain what you meant,' she demanded.

'Let me,' said Jack. 'He thinks you're part of a hallucination he's having – a delusion. He thinks you're just part of a program in a computer . . .'

'I don't understand,' said Beatrice, understandably.

'Don't listen to him,' said Travis, 'he's babbling.'

But Jack, after scratching his head, went on. 'A computer is a machine, kind of like a loom only a bit more complicated . . . and he thinks you're just part of a tapestry that this loom is churning out . . .'

Beatrice stared hard at Travis. 'You think I'm a figure in a *tapestry*?'

He held up his hands. 'No, no, of course not!'

She advanced on him. 'But you don't think I'm real?'

'It's hard to explain . . .'

'You can say that again,' she said, just before she kicked him very hard in the shin of his left leg. 'How about that? Did that feel real to you?'

Travis, jumping about on his right leg while holding his throbbing left one, cried, 'Ow, ow, ow . . . yes, the pain is real alright! But that doesn't prove *you* are . . . !'

'You're mad,' she told him.

'Not yet,' he muttered through gritted teeth, 'But I'm getting pretty annoyed.' Above him he could hear Jack cackling with glee.

'I'm a fool,' she said. 'I've thrown my lot in with a crazy man and a putrid demon.'

'Hey, watch it!' cried Jack.

'We didn't exactly twist your arm to make you come with us,' Travis told her angrily. 'And it's not too late to take you back to your father and claim the reward.'

She scowled at the long-stemmed rose that she was still holding, then tossed it into the dying fire. 'No, I'm not going back. I'll stay with you two until I encounter more suitable – and less eccentric – travelling companions. Now I'm going to bed.' She got the blanket from her horse, wrapped herself in it and lay down beside the fire. 'Goodnight,' she muttered as she turned over with her back to them.

'Well, thanks a lot,' Travis hissed at Jack.

'Hey, kid, I've done you a favour,' said Jack quietly as he landed on Travis's shoulder. 'A relationship between you and a babe in a computer program could never have worked out in the long run. I mean, think of the kids you might have produced. They'd have been nothing but a bunch of little glitches.'

Travis batted Jack from his shoulder. The demon flew off into the night, cackling.

Chapter Seven

'Will you *please* say something?' he pleaded.

It was late afternoon and Beatrice hadn't said a thing to him all day. From the moment she'd woken until now she had totally ignored him. She'd even occasionally spoken to Jack, of all people (or whatever), rather than to him, and that had especially hurt. He'd given up trying by lunchtime, but now that Jack was off on another of his scouting trips he thought he'd make one last attempt. 'Please, Beatrice . . .'

She surpised him by looking back over her shoulder, saying 'I don't see why you're bothering to talk to someone you don't believe exists.' Then she faced front again.

Encouraged, he dug his heels into Whiplash's rubs and got him to move up alongside her steed. 'I just want to explain to you . . .'

'If I'm not real, what's the point?' she asked, huffily. 'You might as well just talk to yourself. You probably do a lot of that anyway.'

'Beatrice, when I said you're not real, I meant that you're not real to me outside of this world. Because, to be honest, this whole world often doesn't seem very real.'

'Clear as mud.'

'Look, I told you I came from a different world, didn't I?'

She nodded.

'Well, it's a *very* different world to this one. We don't have things like those elves we encountered last night . . . well, actually we have people *like* them but they're not called elves . . . and we don't have fairies . . . well, we do have people who are sometimes called fairies, usually behind their backs, but they're more like your elves. They don't have wings or fly about . . .' He paused, sighed and gamely kept going. 'We don't have sorcerers or wizards or even magic.' He paused,

'Well, we have people who believe we do but the official, scientific view is that we don't.'

She gave him a disbelieving look. 'How can you have a world that doesn't have *magic*?' she asked, 'It wouldn't make any sense.'

'You're probably right. But anyway, all this . . .' He waved his hand about. '. . . Your world and the things in it are similar to a common mythology we have in our world. People write books about it: they're full of knights, princesses, dragons, sorcerers, witches, magic spells, heroic quests to find the special talisman that will defeat the forces of evil and restore the power of goodness to the land etc etc . . . But these are all fairy stories. They're not real. So when I find myself in this world of yours which kind of mirrors the world of all those books you can understand why I'm, well, not fully convinced that it's real.'

She looked at him for a time in silence. Then she said, 'Have you had any bad falls from your horse recently? You know, hit your head very hard? Such blows can sometimes addle the brain. I knew a page at court who, after a fall, thought he was the King's long-lost son and therefore my brother and the rightful heir to the throne. I fear he still languishes in one of the castle dungeons. Eric is his name. Or rather Prince Eric as he insists on being called.'

'No, I haven't fallen off the damned horse!' he told her angrily. 'Nor have I sustained any serious blows to the head. I'm telling you the truth. I'm trying to explain why I said you didn't seem real to me!'

'Well, I know *I'm* real but I'm beginning to have my doubts about you. How do you know that *you're* not the unreal one around here?'

'That's nonsense! I *know* I'm real . . .'

'Can you prove it?' she asked with a sweet smile.

'I guess not,' he admitted.

'Well, that's that. We'll just have to mutually accept that we're both real on trust. Agreed?'

'Agreed,' he muttered.

'And I'll even pretend I don't believe you to be completely mad.'

'Thanks a lot.'

'You're welcome.'

Just then a shadow fell upon Travis. He looked up to see Jack returning. Jack landed on Whiplash's head, much to the horse's obvious irritation. 'I see you and the royal babe are talking again. How'd you manage that?'

'Never mind. What's up ahead?'

'A fairly big town, and beyond it a damn big castle,' said Jack.

Travis looked at Beatrice. 'Any idea what this place is?'

'We've been travelling north, haven't we?' she asked.

'In that general direction, yeah,' said Jack.

'Then it might be the kingdom of the Black Baron,' she said.

'The Black Baron, eh?' said Jack. 'Sounds like he's a real mean-hearted bastard.'

'On the contrary,' said Beatrice. 'From what I hear he's a kind and just ruler.'

'Then why's called the Black Baron?' asked Jack.

'Because he's black.'

'Oh,' said Jack.

'Then again, if we've been travelling in a north-westerly direction, it could be the kingdom of Prince Valerie,' said Beatrice.

'Prince Valerie,' repeated Travis. 'He's not an elf, is he?'

'No. Why do you ask?'

'Funny name for a bloke. Valerie.'

'What do you mean?'

'Well, where I come from, Valerie is a girl's name.'

'There's nothing girlish about Prince Valerie,' she said firmly.

'You've met him?'

'Only once, two years ago. He paid an official visit to Samella and stayed at my father's castle for the night. He's a very handsome man.' Then she gave a little sigh. Travis didn't like the sound of it.

'He'd know you by sight then?' he asked.

'Of course, but don't worry. If it is his kingdom ahead of us there's little chance we'll encounter him on the way through. And besides, even if we did meet him he wouldn't recognize me. I'm in disguise, remember?'

Travis gave a little sigh of his own. 'How could I forget?'

Beatrice looked around the crowded dining room then gave Travis a smug smile. 'No one suspects a thing,' she whispered. 'The disguise is working perfectly.'

Travis almost choked on a spoonful of rabbit's feet and vegetable soup. None of the other diners – and they were all men – could take their eyes off the Princess. From the moment she'd entered with Travis, Beatrice had become the centre of attention. It wasn't just her startling beauty that transfixed them but also her ludicrous pretence of being a boy. When Travis had asked the inn-keeper for a room for himself and his man-servant the landlord had guffawed loudly, and later gave Travis a nudge of titanic proportions in the ribs, and a knowing wink, and informed him quietly that they were a 'broad-minded lot around here'.

It turned out that they had indeed come upon the kingdom of Prince Valerie. And by sheer misfortune they had entered it when it was playing host to a barbarians' convention. Which explained why the inn, like all the other inns in the town, was so crowded. The dining room was packed with barbarians and the air was heavy with the smell of male sweat and baby oil.

Oblivious to the attention she was attracting, Beatrice kept casting appreciative glances at the various naked and gleaming torsos around her. 'This is so exciting,' she told Travis. 'I've never seen so many gorgeous-looking men in one place before. Look at all those *muscles*! Oooh.'

'Yes. Very impressive,' said Travis sourly but quietly, 'Unfortunately most of their muscles are between their ears.'

'Don't be a sourpuss,' she told him.

'I just don't believe it,' he muttered. 'We have to pick a town that's in the middle of a barbarian convention . . .'

'Well *I* think it's marvellous.'

'I've had encounters with barbarians before. Not good. And here we are faced with a whole damned *convention* of them. We should have kept going.'

'But you said yourself we couldn't. Not until Sir Rodney's horse had been given a new shoe.'

'I know, I know,' he muttered. Her steed had thrown a shoe and the blacksmith had told them that what with all the extra work he had on he wouldn't be able to re-shoe the horse until the following morning. But on the bright side they had already managed to sell most of Sir Rodney's equipment. Apart from his sword. Everyone in town seemed to own at least two . . . *Uh oh* . . .

Travis had been expecting something like this. Or rather, dreading it. One of the barbarians had risen from a nearby table and was approaching their own. He had a wide leer on his even wider face. His companions at the table were watching expectantly. At a rough guess Travis placed the approaching barbarian as the biggest man in the room. Which made him very large indeed.

He pulled up a chair – dumping its previous, and much smaller, occupant from it along the way – and sat down at their table. 'Mind if I join you?' he rumbled. He was just one gleaming mass of biceps and pectorals. And his forehead was all of an inch in length.

'Not at all,' said Travis, dropping his hand to the automatic.

'They call me Bovrol,' said the giant, turning his leer onto Beatrice. 'Bovrol the Brutal.'

'I'm sure they do,' Travis told him.

'Thought I'd buy you and your *boy* here a drink . . .' There were sniggers from all directions. He turned back to Travis. 'That okay?'

'Sure,' said Travis.

Bovrol the Barbarian signalled an order to the landlord, who broke all records in getting three tankards of ale to their table, and then insisted they were on the house. Travis could sense trouble looming ahead on the horizon like a giant, smelly turd.

'Go on, *boy*, drink,' the giant ordered Beatrice.

Beatrice was regarding the tankard, a medium-sized bucket, with alarm. 'Er, not just now, thanks. Maybe later.'

Her efforts to lower her voice were so ludicrous Travis would have laughed out loud if he hadn't felt more like having a crying fit.

'I insist, *boy*,' growled Bovrol. More sniggers from the surrounding tables.

Travis knew he had no choice but to say something. After an inward sigh, he said, 'I'm – ah – sure young Andy is grateful but he can't drink alcohol. He's . . . under age.' Then picked up his own tankard, which wasn't easy, and began to drink. He was surprised when the giant plucked it out of his hands and then poured it over himself. Then he slammed the tankard on the table and cried accusingly to Travis, 'You did that on purpose!'

Travis stared stupidly at the barbarian who was now dripping with ale. 'No I didn't. You did that to yourself.'

The giant looked around. 'Did anyone else see this little rat's dropping throw his drink over me?'

There were rapidly nodding heads in all directions. Travis drew the .45, keeping it hidden under the table.

Bovrol turned to Travis, 'For this insult I challenge you to a duel to the death in the convention arena tomorrow at noon. The weapons will be broadswords. The victor, as is the custom, gets all the worldly goods of the loser. And that includes *him*.' He nodded towards Beatrice, then rose to his feet. Travis was surprised that clouds weren't forming around his head, it was now so far away. 'You'd better be there, or every barbarian in the land will be out to hunt you down.' Then he strode back to his own table.

Amid laughter and chuckles the other barbarians resumed their eating and drinking.

Beatrice hissed at Travis. 'Why didn't you use your talisman on the brute?'

'It may have escpaed your attention but I'm kind of outnumbered in here.'

'So what will you do?'

'I assure you I'm going to give the matter a great deal of serious thought over the next few hours,' he told her as he reholstered the gun.

'You can't fight him in a fair duel,' she protested, 'You'd be killed. And I don't want to end up belonging to that . . . *barbarian*!'

'Well, if the worst comes to the worst, just lie back and think of all those muscles,' he told her.

Chapter Eight

'I'm in trouble,' said Travis.

'Tell me something I don't know,' replied Jack. The demon was reclining on Whiplash's back and smoking one of his Marlboros.

Travis told him what had happened in the inn. He wasn't too surprised by the demon's response, which was to roll on his back, cackling, and kick his little legs into the air with glee.

'I knew I could depend on your sympathy,' said Travis.

When Jack had calmed down he said, 'My advice is that we make tracks, pronto. The barbarians won't try and track you down until their stupid convention's over, and that's four days from now. Gives us plenty of time to make a long head-start.'

'I'd like to do just that but they wouldn't let Beatrice leave the inn with me.'

'All the better. If the barbarian who challenged you gets what he wants, which is obviously her, then he and the others are less likely to chase after you.'

He shook his head. 'I can't abandon Beatrice. Not to Bogroll.'

'Bogroll?'

'His real name is Bovrol. Bovrol the Brutal. But I prefer to call him Bogroll. You wouldn't understand. It's a British thing.'

'Look, she's not your responsibility. The stupid babe insisted on coming along even though we both warned her it would be tough. Besides . . .' And he sniggered evilly. '. . . She wanted adventure. Well, she's gonna get it – in spades. The way those barbarians make love she's gonna be walking bow-legged for life.'

Travis regarded Jack with distaste. 'You're disgusting.'

'I know. It's my job.'

'I'm not leaving her here,' said Travis firmly.

'So instead you're gonna get chopped into small pieces tomorrow in the arena. How's that going to help her?'

Travis slowly rubbed his chin. 'I'm going to have to figure out something very clever.'

'You're goddamned doomed then.'

'I beat that dragon, didn't I?'

'Pure luck. Look, I've got an idea . . . why don't you find out where this Bovrol guy is sleeping tonight, creep up on him and blow his brains out?'

'It has its appeal, I admit,' said Travis. 'But it's hardly the honourable thing to do.'

'Screw honour,' said Jack, tossing his butt away. It landed in some straw which immediately started to smoulder. Travis ran over to the fledgling fire and stamped it out. 'The other drawback to that idea is that his barbarian buddies will know it was me and I'd still end up as little pieces of meat.' He glared at the demon.

'Yeah. Hmmm, it's sure a problem,' agreed Jack.

'Got any other ideas?'

'How about the old poison-on-the-tip-of-your-sword routine?'

'The what?'

'You put poison on the tip of your sword. All you have to do is get close enough to just nick your opponent and when he starts to slow down from the effects of the stuff you move in and finish him off.'

'Oh, I see. You got that from *Hamlet*, did you?'

'Nah, from a guy called Derek. A professional cut-throat I met once.'

'Well, I don't think it would work. My chances of getting close enough to even nick Bogroll are pretty remote. His arms are longer than my legs. And twice as thick.'

'You're going to have to use ol' Sir Rodney's sword then,' said Jack. 'Your rapier's far too short.'

Travis went over to the sword that was leaning against the stable wall. He picked it up, grunting from the effort. Even using both hands he could hardly keep it raised. 'If I try and use this the duel will be over in seconds. Besides, where am I going to get poison at this time of night? All the shops are closed.'

'Dickwit, you'd better come up with something real clever by tomorrow or the Princess babe is gonna become an ex-virgin in a hell of a big way as soon as you bite the dust. Speaking of who, you think she's safe back there in the inn on her own?'

'Yes. The other barbarians already think she's Bogroll's property so they won't bother her. And he's happy to wait until tomorrow before he claims her. Barbarian honour, so I'm told. She's safe enough in our room.'

'*Our* room?' sniggered Jack. 'You and the babe are sharing?'

'We have no choice. There was only one room available. And we were lucky to get that. There was a last minute cancellation. The barbarian who'd booked it got torn apart by a bunch of trolls at the end of a quest.'

'So maybe she won't still be a virgin when your Bogroll buddy claims his prize tomorrow.'

'Don't be ridiculous. I'm going to be too worried to even sleep, much less attempt a seduction.' But actually, Travis, despite all his anxieties about what was going to happen the next day, *was* thinking of what might possibly happen in their room tonight.

He knocked on the door.

'Who is it?' Beatrice called, sounding nervous.

'It's me. Travis.'

'How can I be sure it's really you?'

'Trust me, Beatrice. It's really me. Open the door.'

'It could be a trick.'

He sighed. 'Yes, it's a trick. I'm really Bovrol the Brutal doing a clever voice imitation of Travis. Now open this bloody door before I break it open with a blow of my mighty nose!'

After a few moments he heard her unbar the door. He

pushed it open and went in. 'Surprise! It really was me after all,' he told her.

She was standing there in just her shirt. Or rather, in Sir Rodney's shirt. All Travis's feelings of annoyance towards her immediately vanished, to be replaced by other ones. He shut the door and barred it. 'Any trouble while I was gone?' he asked.

She walked over to the bed and sat down. The hem of the shirt rode up on her smooth, white thighs. He swallowed and wondered if she shaved her legs.

'No,' she told him.

'You don't?' he asked, startled that she had read his mind.

'What?' she said, frowning.

He realized that she was answering his spoken question rather than the unspoken. 'Oh, good,' he said quickly.

'Except for when a few barbarians gathered outside and sang a bawdy song.'

'They did? What about?'

'It was a song about the size of Bovrol's organ. According to the lyrics, which were quite clever actually, it's of enormous size. Even allowing for a certain amount of exaggeration I'm in for a very uncomfortable time if I should fall into his clutches tomorrow.' She gave him an imploring look. 'You've *got* to do something, otherwise I'll have to kill myself.' Her eyes filled with tears.

He sat down beside her on the bed and, tentatively, put his arm around her shoulder. 'Don't worry, I'll get us out of this mess. Somehow.'

'How?'

'I'm still working on it,' he admitted. 'A few details still to be ironed out on the master plan.'

'You *have* a plan then?'

'Sort of.'

He felt her shoulders sag. 'No you don't. And that barbarian is going to kill you.'

'No he won't,' he said, wishing he felt as confident as he sounded.

'He will,' she said dolefully. 'You can't possibly beat him in a sword fight. I can't see why you won't use your talisman on him.'

'I told you. Rules. You can't use magic in an official barbarian duel. And my gun would be considered magic. Which I suppose it is, of course . . ' He sighed. 'If the worst comes to the worst I *will* use it on him,' he promised her. 'Then I'll try and shoot our way out of there but I can't guarantee I'll succeed.' In reality he knew he wouldn't have a hope. 'But at least Bovrol will be dead.'

She leaned her head against his shoulder. 'And if you die as well some other barbarian will claim me.'

Travis's mind was emptier than an early morning TV presenter's, so he didn't say anything. And Travis couldn't help himself – he felt guilty about it under the circumstances, but the feel of her body against his, the warmth, her scent, caused him to become excited. He tried to think of other things. It didn't work. Then he thought of facing Bovrol in the arena and his growing erection quickly began to recede.

'Well, let's go to bed,' said Beatrice.

His member immediately changed direction. 'Sure,' he said eagerly. 'What side of the bed do you want?'

She pulled away and stared at him in amazement. 'You thought we were going to sleep in the *same* bed?' she asked, disbelievingly.

He looked around the room then said, 'As far as I can see there *is* only one bed in here.'

She stood up. 'You will be sleeping there,' she pointed at the floor beside the bed. 'I put some extra straw down for you.'

Travis looked at the floor. He couldn't detect a place where there was noticeably more straw than any other. 'You expect me to sleep on the bloody *floor*?'

'Of course,' she told him.

He began to feel angry. 'Look, if you thought I was going to try anything with you you couldn't be more wrong.' His erection was completely gone now. 'You can trust me.'

'I'm sure I can trust you, Travis, but that's not the point.'

'Then what *is* the point?' he demanded.

'It wouldn't be proper for us to share a bed together.'

'Why not?'

'Why Travis,' she said, as if puzzled at having to explain something that should be so obvious, 'I'm a princess. And you're just a *commoner*.'

'From the look of you – which is shitty – you clearly didn't sleep a wink last night,' said Jack, smirking on top of one of the stable's rafters, 'so I guess the condemned man enjoyed a good meal. Babe on toast, eh?'

'You're right, I didn't sleep at all,' said Travis as he threw the saddle blanket over Whiplash, 'but no, it wasn't because of what you're thinking. I slept on the floor. Or rather, I *lay* on the floor.'

'She didn't come across? Or were you playing the gentleman?'

Travis picked up the saddle and put it on the horse's back. He began doing up the cinches. 'She *made* me spend the night on the floor. I'm not good enough to be in the same bed with her. She's a bloody princess and I'm just a damned *commoner*.'

'You're kidding! She really say that?' laughed Jack. 'Hey, what are you doing?'

'What does it look like? I'm saddling up Whiplash. We're getting out of here. Now.'

Jack flew down from the rafter and landed on Whiplash's head. 'We are? What about the babe Princess?'

'That stuck-up cow is now on her own. And good luck to her. I hope she and Bogroll will be very happy together.'

'Now you're cooking with gas,' said Jack. 'You're talking sense at last. I told you she was going to be nothing but trouble.'

Travis strapped on his saddlebags to the horse. 'Yes, I admit, you were right. Why should I risk my life for someone who's not even real in the first place?' He climbed into the saddle and took the reins. Then he paused.

'So what are you waiting for?' Jack asked. 'Let's get going.'

'Damn,' muttered Travis.

'What's wrong?' asked Jack.

Travis reluctantly dismounted. 'I can't do it. I can't leave her. I'm going to have to show up at the arena.'

'Are you crazy? You just said you didn't even think she was real? And now you're gonna fight a *duel* over her? A duel with a guy who makes Arnold Schwarzenegger look anorexic?'

'I'm not a hundred percent certain she's *not* real. And if there's even a small chance she *is* real I'm not going to abandon her to that moron of a barbarian without a fight.'

'A man's gotta do what a man's gotta do, eh?' sneered Jack. 'This is more a case of a dickwit having to do what a dickwit has to do. You're going to end up as hamburger filling and then what's going to happen to me?'

'I'm sorry, Jack. I'm going. But if you want to help, try and come up with something that might give me an extra edge.'

Scowling, Jack produced a cigarette and lit it. He puffed on it furiously then said, 'I have an idea . . .'

'Gosh, I've suddenly gone tingly all over.'

'You want to hear what it is or do you just want to keep playing smart-ass?'

Travis sighed. 'Yes, I'm *that* desperate.'

And Jack began to tell him his idea . . .

Chapter Nine

The banner read 'Welcome to the 39th Annual Barbarian Convention – sponsored by His Highness Prince Valerie (catering by Fancy Fred's Foodshop)'. The venue was a temporary wooden construction in a field on the edge of town. It was surrounded by stalls selling a variety of drinks, delicacies (Travis noted that the stall selling Smoked Goat's Testicle on a Stick was doing a roaring trade), souvenirs, such as shrunken troll heads, and baby oil. With Jack sitting on his shoulder, Travis went to the Players Entrance. A guard in the doorway barred his way with a rusty spear.

'Where do you think you're going, sunshine?' the man demanded. He was middle-aged and had a small, grey moustache.

'Inside. I'm a contestant,' Travis told him briskly.

The guard looked him up and down with thinly veiled contempt. 'Pull the other one, sunshine. If you're a barbarian I'm a bleeding elf.'

'That wouldn't surprise me one bit,' said Jack.

'I'm not a barbarian but I am a contestant,' Travis told the guard. 'I'm fighting a duel with a barbarian called Bovrol the Brutal. A personal matter. So let me pass. I'm on at noon.'

The guard didn't shift. 'Be more than my job's worth to let you in just on your say-so. Got any proof?'

Travis groaned. Jack said. 'I can vouch that this man is a sad, mad suicidal dickwit. Would any sane man turn up to fight a duel to the death with some asshole of a barbarian called Bovrol the Brutal?'

The guard thought it over. 'Hmmm, you have a point, demon.'

'Thank you, Jack,' said Travis, dryly.

The guard stood aside and let them enter. After giving Travis directions to the changing room he said 'Good luck, squire. No offence, of course, but I'm just off to place a bet on your duel. And I think you know who I'll be putting my money on.'

Travis didn't say anything. The changing room turned out to be a large place full of wooden benches and lockers. Barbarians in various stages of undress either lounged about getting messages from their trainers, sat sharpening their weapons or were doing warm-up exercises. The air was full of the smell of jock straps and male hormones. As Travis entered someone nearby cried, 'Hey, you can't bring that demon in here!'

'I have to. He's my coach,' said Travis and continued on.

Beatrice, who had been escorted to the arena earlier by two of Bovrol's companions, emerged from the thonged throng looking distraught. With her long hair falling out from under her cap and her more than obvious femininity, she looked as out of place in this aggressively all-male environment as Bambi at a wolves convention. Though still angry, he couldn't help feeling sorry for her. But not as sorry as he was feeling for himself.

'Travis, I was beginning to think you weren't going to turn up!'

'I almost didn't, *Princess*. I had an attack of sanity but unfortunately it passed off.'

She gazed at his empty hands with a stricken expression. 'Where's Sir Rodney's sword?'

'In the stable. I'm suffering under enough handicaps without adding a double hernia to the list.'

'But what are you going to fight Bovrol with?' she cried.

He patted the rapier that hung by his side. 'This.'

She looked more stricken. 'But you can't with that little thing! Have you seen the *size* of Bovrol's?!'

'Hah!' laughed Jack.

'Please, I'm feeling inadequate enough as it is,' Travis told her. 'But don't worry – I have something up my sleeve. I hope.'

'Like what?' she asked worriedly.

Just then Bovrol lumbered into view, looking even larger

than he had on the previous evening. Travis immediately assumed a heroic stance and boomed as authoritively as he could: 'So Bovrol, you dared to show your cowardly face here today!'

Bovrol's face clouded over. 'I was going to say that,' he complained.

'I know,' said Travis.

An elderly greybeard, wearing a long green robe and carrying a wooden staff, appeared at Bovrol's elbow. He introduced himself as the Master of Ceremonies and said, 'And you, sir, would be Bovrol's vict . . . er, opponent?'

'I'm afraid so,' admitted Travis.

'Well, young man, you should be feeling very fortunate today,' said the MC.

'I should?' asked Travis, surprised. Had Bovrol pulled a hamstring? Was he withdrawing from the duel?

No such luck.

'Normally only barbarians would be allowed to take part in the Games, but in your case we're making a special exception,' the MC told him.

'Hey, there's no need to go to any trouble on my behalf,' said Travis quickly, 'I don't want to cause a problem . . .'

The MC held up a hand. 'It's no problem. Bovrol himself came up with the solution. We're going to make you an honorary barbarian for the hour . . . er, day. What do you think of that?'

Travis wanted to say what he really thought of the idea but instead he said, 'I'm so overcome with gratitude I'm speechless . . . Good old Bovrol.'

From out of the arena a great cheer arose from the crowd. 'Ah,' said the MC, 'that means the hydra's lost another head to Rupert the Rampant. Five down and two to go. You're on next so we'd better hurry. Any preference for your name?'

'Uh?' said Travis, blankly.

'You have to have a proper barbarian's name,' explained the MC. 'You know, like Bovrol the Brutal. It has to be Travis the "something". Do you have a preference?'

Various possibilities occurred to Travis. 'Travis the

Torpid', 'Travis the Soon-to-be-Deceased', 'Travis the Incredibly Stupid', 'Travis the Trivial' . . . He said, 'How about "Travis the Politically Incorrect"?'

The MC frowned. 'It doesn't sound very heroic to me? What does it mean?'

'Believe me, where I come from it takes a great deal of heroism to be described as Politically Incorrect.'

'Oh very well,' said the MC. 'We're running out of time. Bow your head.'

Travis did so. The MC touched him on the top of his head with his staff and intoned. 'I dub you Travis the Politically Incorrect, honorary barbarian for the day. Prepare yourself. That cheer means the hydra is down to one head. Won't be long now.'

Travis shooed Jack from off his shoulder and began taking off his jacket. 'Hey,' cried Bovrol, 'Where's your sword?'

'Right here,' replied Travis, indicating the rapier.

'You call that dinky little thing a *sword*?' sneered Bovrol. 'The duel was to be fought with broadswords.'

'You making an official complaint, Bovrol?' asked the MC.

'Yes. Surely you're not afraid I can do you any damage with this dinky little thing,' said Travis as he removed his shirt.

Bovrol scratched his head doubtfully. It was clear that mental activity didn't come easy for him. Thinking wasn't just an uphill struggle, it was a major mountaineering expedition. 'Well, I guess I don't have any complaints,' he said at last.

'Good,' said Travis. 'Now let's get this show on the road.' He glanced around and flexed his muscles. 'Anyone care to lend me a cup of baby oil?'

Travis followed Bovrol out into the arena. Just before he'd left the changing room Beatrice had whispered into his ear, 'Good luck, Travis, and don't forget, I've a lot riding on this duel.' *Yes*, he thought, *and if I lose it you're going to have a lot riding on you*. 'I'll do my best,' he told her. 'Then we're all doomed,' said Jack from his perch on the window sill.

Travis gave him the finger and left.

The arena was littered with hydra heads. They were incredibly ugly. One of them blinked at Travis as he accompanied Bovrol and the MC out to the centre of the sand-filled arena. The tiers of seats lining the circular amphitheatre were packed with spectators.

When they reached the centre of the sand-covered, and blood-splattered, arena the MC said, 'Bow to the Royal Box,' and bowed in the direction of a separate seating area covered with bunting and regal-looking flags. Travis and Bovrol did the same. Then the MC began to speak out loudly: 'Your Royal Highness, fellow barbarians, ladies and gentlemen and all other types of creatures present, it is my pleasure to announce this grudge duel between Bovrol the Barbarian's Barbarian and Travis the Politically Incorrect!' A ripple of polite applause came from the crowd.

'Now, fellows,' said the MC, conversationally, 'you know the rules. There aren't any apart from the banning of any form of magic. And for goodness sakes, Bovrol, drag this thing out a bit. The crowd isn't going to like it if you butcher this poor fool in the opening few seconds.'

'Don't worry,' Bovrol told him, 'his death will be a slow and painful one.'

'Glad to hear it,' said the MC. 'Now I'm out of here. Start the duel when I'm in the clear.'

As the MC sprinted back towards the changing room door, Travis and Bovrol faced each other and drew their swords. The crowd laughed when they saw the size of Travis's weapon. Travis began to back away from Bovrol. The giant sneered at him. 'Where do you think you're going, pygmy?'

Travis kept backing away. He could feel a panic attack coming on but he told himself to try and stay calm. He wished he was anywhere else but there in the arena facing Bovrol. Even being stuck in a rush-hour tube carriage on the Northern Line would have been preferable.

Well, no, things weren't quite *that* bad.

Using one hand, Bovrol swished his broadsword, which

seemed to be about fifty feet long, through the air. The shock-wave almost knocked Travis over.

Bovrol began to advance on Travis. Travis tossed his rapier up, let go of it then grabbed it again around the shaft near the hilt. He drew his arm back and then hurled it with all his strength at Bovrol. The barbarian had no chance of deflecting the fast moving rapier with his massive sword. The rapier sunk deep into Bovrol's left, baby-oiled pectoral.

'Oof,' said Bovrol and came to a halt. A shocked gasp rose from the spectators. The barbarian started to sway backwards and forwards. He reached up with his free hand and pulled the rapier from his chest. Blood began to pour from the wound. He dropped the rapier, then, after a few more moments of swaying, fell backwards into the sand. There was a very loud thud, then all was silence.

Bloody hell! It worked! thought Travis.

Someone in the audience booed, but then someone else cheered. There were more boos but very soon the sound of cheering drowned them out. Travis took a deep breath and exhaled slowly. Against all the odds he had beaten Bovrol. Okay, his method may not have been exactly kosher but the MC himself had said there were no rules. He had *won*, clear and simple.

And then Bovrol suddenly sat up, got to his feet and with a bellow of rage, charged towards Travis.

What a bloody spoilsport, thought Travis as he ran frantically to avoid falling into Bovrol's clutches.

It's okay, he told himself, *this is just a dying reflex on Bovrol's part. Like a chicken after its head's been chopped off. The sword must have penetrated his heart. Very soon he'll drop dead properly. All you have to do is keep going . . .*

By the fifth circuit of the arena's perimeter, accompanied by cheers and hoots of laughter from the spectators, Travis was beginning to think that, like Bovrol, his theory had a serious hole in it.

Then he tripped over one of the hydra's heads and fell on his face. 'Bollocks,' he groaned. Behind him he could hear the thunder of Bovrol's heavy, approaching tread. He had no choice . . .

He rolled over onto his back, drawing the Colt .45 as he did so. He shot the charging giant three times and Bovrol crashed into the ground beside him. This time he was definitely dead, but Travis knew, with the final shot still echoing around the arena, that his problems had only just begun.

At first there was a stunned silence and then pandemonium erupted. Among the roar of disapproval Travis heard the words 'Cheat!' and 'Sorcery!' He got to his feet and looked around. The spectators had all risen – apart from those in the Royal Box, which was nearby – and were shaking their fists at them. Some began to throw fruit at him. A half-eaten apple hit him in his chest. He saw the MC coming across the arena towards him, followed by a group of angry-looking barbarians. Beatrice was among them.

'What dastardly act of magic did you just use to fell Bovrol?!' demanded the MC furiously when he arrived.

'It wasn't magic, exactly,' protested Travis, knowing it was a waste of time, 'It's a new kind of weapon.'

'It looked and sounded like magic to me,' said the MC. 'Give me that thing!'

Travis shook his head. 'Sorry,' and pointed the gun at him. 'I can do to you what I did to Bovrol. But please don't make me.'

Then Beatrice arrived, with the group of angry barbarians not far behind her. She flung her arms around him. 'Oh Travis, you did it! You saved me from him!'

'Please, not now,' he said, quickly disentangling himself from her arms. They were now ringed by shouting barbarians, most of whom were carrying weapons. 'And we're not exactly out of the woods yet,' he told her. He raised the gun into the air and fired it several times. He had the wild hope they would scatter in panic at the sound like primitive natives in some old Hollywood movie. They didn't. There was silence for a time as the barbarians backed away a short distance and then someone said accusingly, 'The dirty cheat makes more magic!'

'He says it's a new kind of weapon,' said the MC.

'Yes, it is!' cried Travis. 'It's kind of like a small crossbow . . . which shoots very small arrows,' he finished lamely.

'It's magic!' cried a barbarian. 'And even if it's not, it's surely not a sword. The duel was to have been fought by swords, right?'

'Yes,' agreed the MC. 'He did not fight the duel according to the rules and the penalty must be death. The girl, his servant, will become the common property of the Guild of Barbarians.'

Travis put his arm around her waist and moved the gun back and forth. 'I'll kill the first man who makes a move towards us,' he warned them, but he knew the position was hopeless. He could kill a few of them but he would be quickly overwhelmed by the others.

And what would happen to Beatrice afterwards didn't bear thinking about.

Chapter Ten

Beatrice pulled off her cap, shook her hair loose, drew her shoulders back and stood very straight. 'Harken to me,' she said loudly. 'I am Princess Beatrice, daughter of the King of Vallium! Lay a finger on either myself or my companion and you will pay dearly!'

Her words produced a lot of sniggering. One barbarian said, 'You a princess? Pull the other leg, darling, it's covered in baby oil.'

'Yes,' said the MC. 'Why in the world would a princess be travelling with this dubious knave – and dressed like a boy? Not that the disguise is in the least bit convincing.'

'You can say that again,' said another barbarian, leering at her. 'My *sister* looks more like a boy than she does. Mind you, sis does have a moustache.'

'I tell you I am Princess Beatrice!' she cried, just as two armoured soldiers pushed their way through the crowd. 'Prince Valerie wants to know what's going on!' said one of them.

'I've just sentenced this man to death for using sorcery on Bovrol but now his female companion is claiming to be royalty. A Princess Beatrice of Vallium . . .'

'By the gods, so it is!' The speaker had just appeared behind the two soldiers. He was a tall, handsome man with saturnine features. From the finery of his costume it was clear to Travis that this had to be the Prince. He was followed by a younger man – not much more than a youth – dressed entirely in black. The Prince came up to Beatrice and smiled at her. 'Yes, it definitely is you. You've grown some since I last saw you and have become even more beautiful in the process.'

Beatrice blushed. 'I'm so relieved you recognize me, Prince Valerie.'

'It would take a man of extremely dulled senses to ever forget one such as you,' he said as he took her hand and kissed it. *Good grief*, thought Travis. 'But what are you doing here dressed in that outlandish way, and in the company of this man?' He glanced briefly at Travis.

'It would take some time to explain,' said Beatrice. 'But first can you do something to help Travis? They want to kill him.'

'For cheating, Your Highness,' said the MC. 'That thing in his hand is some kind of magical device. You yourself must have seen him use it to kill Bovrol.'

The Prince turned to Travis. 'What have you got to say about this?'

Travis tried to think of something really clever, but found he was suffering from a severe shortage of inspiration. 'It's a weapon,' he told the Prince, 'but the only magical thing about it is that it doesn't run out of bullets. Those are the things it fires. Bovrol has three of them inside him, which is what killed him . . .'

The youthful-looking man spoke for the first time. 'May I see it?' he asked, holding out his hand. Travis put the gun on 'safety' and reluctantly gave it to him. The man held it in both his hands and studied it with a frown.

'What do you think, Damion?' the Prince asked him.

'It has a strange aura to it. A powerful one. And it's not of this world.'

'That's right!' said Beatrice, eagerly. 'Travis comes from another world.'

'You do?' the youth asked him, regarding him with intense interest, 'What's it called and where is it?'

'It's called Earth. As for directions, that's kind of difficult.'

'And how did you travel to our world?' Prince Valerie asked him.

'By magic,' admitted Travis.

'See? He admits he uses sorcery!' thundered the MC. 'I demand that my judgment upon him be carried out!'

'Oh no!' cried Beatrice, and took hold of the Prince's hand. 'Please do something, I beg you! Travis saved my life. And more!'

'Did he really?' asked the Prince. 'Then that puts a different complexion on the matter. Any man who has saved your life has earned my profound gratitude.' He turned to the MC. 'I'm commuting his sentence. Besides, he is a stranger here and clearly not familiar with our customs. And by the look of it, Bovrol shouldn't have challenged him in the first place. It was obviously a mis-match.'

The MC opened his mouth to protest but quickly closed it again. There were a few muted mutters from the surrounding barbarians but no one made any outright protests. Travis could see that the Prince's word was law.

The Prince bowed to Beatrice and said, 'You and your protector are to be my guests at the castle. We shall leave now, in my carriage.'

'Thank you, Prince Valerie,' said Beatrice, blushing again.

'Yes, thanks,' said Travis, feeling intensely relieved, 'But first do you mind if I just go and pick up the rest of my clothing? And there's something else – I have this demon . . .'

'Don't we all?' sighed the Prince.

'No, he's a real demon. Name of Jack. I'll try and explain later why he has to travel with me. Okay, if I go and fetch him?'

'Of course. One of my men will escort you to where the carriage is waiting.'

'Fine.' Travis turned to the young man and held out his hand for the gun. But the Prince shook his head. 'No, I think it best if your curious weapon remains with Damion for the time being.'

'Oh,' said Travis. He didn't like this development one little bit.

Some fifteen minutes later Travis was riding in Prince Valerie's opulent carriage, drawn by four white horses, in the company of the Prince himself, Beatrice and the mysterious Damion. Jack had been banished to the roof of the carriage, much to his disgust. The Princess and Valerie were sitting side by side and, much to Travis's disgust, she was clearly relishing his company. Beside Travis sat Damion who was still examining the Colt .45 with interest. 'Are you a relative of the Prince's?' Travis asked him politely.

'Me? No, I'm the court wizard.'

'You are?' said Travis, surprised. 'Awfully young to be a wizard, aren't you?'

'Not all wizards have to be grey-haired old men with long beards, you know,' the youth said huffily. 'We all have to start off sometime. I graduated from the College of the Dark Arts just last year. This is my first posting.'

'Interesting work?'

'Very. The Prince is an ideal employer. And the long-term prospects are good.'

'So what does a court wizard do exactly? Amuse the Prince and his courtiers with card tricks – that kind of thing?'

'I do not!' said the young man rather sharply. 'My work involves protecting the Prince from those who would use evil magic against him.'

'Oh, I see,' said Travis, 'and are you kept busy?'

Damion nodded. 'My liege has many enemies.'

Travis pondered on this. His impression so far of Prince Valerie was that he was a genial man. But then he supposed that even the most benevolent of rulers attracted enemies.

'There it is!' announced the Prince, proudly, as he pointed out the window. 'Castle Drysfillia!'

Travis looked out and saw, in the distance, a huge white structure that was all tall gleaming turrets and spires. A *proper* castle at last. It even had a moat and a drawbridge. 'It's magnificent,' he told the Prince. 'Must have cost you a bomb to build.'

'A bomb?' asked the Prince, raising an eyebrow.

'A fortune.'

'Drysfillia has belonged to my family for generations. It was originally built by my great, great grandfather, Lord Brian the Brazen. Extensions have been added to it over the years, of course. I myself was responsible for the recent construction of that tower on the east wing. It will be for my bride.'

'Oh, you're getting married then?'

'When I find the right woman,' the Prince replied and glanced meaningfully at Beatrice, who blushed again.

Travis sighed inwardly.

'Something smells,' said Jack.

'Yes, it's you,' Travis told him.

'I mean Prince Val. I think there's something funny about him. And I don't trust his little pal either.' Jack was sitting in the alcove of a narrow window and smoking one of his Marlboros.

'I'm with you there, but the Prince seems okay. And he's certainly lavish with his hospitality. This is the best room I've been in since arriving on this stupid planet. Not a piece of straw in sight and genuine linen on the bed. And as for this bath, sheer bliss.' Servants had arrived half an hour ago carrying a large, round wooden tub and had then proceeded to fill it with hot water. Travis was still reclining in it, soaking away the aches and tiredness from his over-strained muscles.

'Well, my nose tells me there's something not quite right about the Prince,' said Jack. 'I mean, what kind of guy goes around calling hmself *Valerie*? Prince Valiant – yeah, that's a name that makes sense, but not Prince Valerie.'

'If you're suggesting he's gay then he's doing a good job of disguising the fact. It's more than clear he fancies Beatrice.'

'Yeah, I guess so. And the babe has got the hots for him too.'

'Don't I know it,' said Travis sourly.

There was a knock on the door. Travis called 'Come in!' and a young, very pale but attractive servant girl entered carrying an armful of clothing. She gave Travis a curtsey and said, 'Prince Valerie asked me to bring you this change of clothing, sir.'

'Fine,' said Travis, 'just lay everything out on the bed.'

'Including yourself,' said Jack to the girl and sniggered.

She pretended not to hear the demon's remark. She placed a pair of soft-leather boots on the floor and laid out the suit of clothes on the bed. Then she picked up one of the large white towels that the other servants had left and held it out. 'If you'd care to step from the bath I shall dry you, sir,' she said.

Travis, surprised, said, 'That won't be necessary but thanks all the same.'

'I have my instructions, sir,' she told him, 'and I must always obey the Prince.'

'Oh,' said Travis, studying her. She was aged about eighteen, had jet black hair tied in braids and had large, soulful eyes. 'Er, well, fine,' he said, 'I wouldn't want to get you into trouble.'

Jack laughed. 'This I have got to see,' he said.

'Jack, why don't you go and check out the moat?'

Travis was admiring himself in the mirror when Jack returned.

'Coast clear? You've finished playing your naughty games with the hired help?'

'Your foul suspicions are completely wrong. It was all perfectly innocent. She just dried me, helped me dress then left.'

'Oh yeah, sure.'

'It's true, believe me.'

'And just how innocent were your thoughts while she was drying you off, eh?'

'Not entirely innocent, I admit, but she's just a girl and I was certainly not going to take advantage of her.'

'You're so noble you make me ill.'

'Glad to hear it. Anyway, how do I look?' He turned around, showing off his new clothes.

'Want the truth? You look like you're off to audition for an all-girl musical version of *Peter Pan*.'

'Yes, it's a bit over the top, I admit, but at least these clothes are *clean* and the underwear doesn't feel as if it was made out of straw. Well, I'm off to dinner. Want me to bring you anything back? I doubt if goats' testicle stew is on the menu here but I'm sure I can find you something suitable.'

'Nah, don't bother. I've already eaten. The castle refuse

pipes empty out into the moat and there were all kinds of interesting things floating around down there.'

'Thanks Jack. There goes my appetite.'

But Travis had regained it by the time the food started being served in the royal dining hall. As he'd expected, the food was good and included soups, venison, chicken, roast potatoes, a variety of vegetables and copious quantities of good red wine. He was less satisfied with the seating arrangements. While Beatrice – looking stunning in a low-cut red gown studded with jewels – sat at the head table next to the Prince, Travis was relegated to one of the two side tables. He was stuck between a fat man, who was an extraordinarily messy eater, and Damion who plagued him with endless questions about his home world. Damion also asked him for a demonstration of the gun in the courtyard the following morning after breakfast. Travis had no choice but to agree.

Another source of irritation was the sight of the Prince and Beatrice together. Whatever gush he kept whispering in her ear she was clearly lapping it up like a cat attacking a dish of cream spiked with catnip. She kept giggling and blushing, and in general acting like a complete prat. Well, no, Travis had to admit to himself, reluctantly and jealously, she was acting like an infatuated young woman. And she didn't glance in Travis's direction even once. Him, her saviour! What ingratitude! What fickleness!

When the dinner was over, disappointed that he hadn't had the opportunity to exchange even a few words with Beatrice, and awash with red wine, Travis made his way unsteadily back to his room. He was relieved to see, when he entered, that Jack was absent. Travis wasn't in the mood right now for dealing with the little sod. But then he never was.

He undressed, put on the sleeping gown that had been laid out for him in his absence – that dark-haired servant-girl again? – and got into the bed. He was about to blow out the candle on the table beside the bed when there came a gentle tapping on the door. *Beatrice*, he thought happily and quickly got out of bed and went to the door.

But it wasn't Beatrice, he saw to his disappointment when he opened the door, it was the pale, black-haired servant girl, a candle holder, with a lit candle, in her hand. She too was wearing a sleeping gown. And her hair was no longer braided. It hung down to her shoulders. 'May I come in, sir?' she asked quietly.

'Yes, of course . . .' He stood aside and she entered. Going to the bed, she put her candle down beside the other one on the table then turned and faced him.

He closed the door. 'Can I help you?' he asked, lamely.

For an answer she pulled the gown up over her head and dropped the garment on the floor. She stood there completely naked, apart from a black ribbon around her neck, and stared silently at him. Like her face, her slim body was very white, except for the jet black triangle of pubic hair which matched the hair on her head. It was a very nice body. The nipples on her small but globular breasts, he noted, were very pink.

He swallowed and said, 'Look, this is all very nice and I appreciate the gesture but I couldn't possibly . . . so please put your robe back on.'

'The Prince has asked me to pleasure you. I must obey him,' she said solemnly.

'Well, I hardly thought for a moment you were doing this of your own volition, but be that as it may, I must refuse his kind offer. Please give him my thanks when you next see him.'

'Why do you refuse his gift?' she asked, in the same solemn voice. 'He will be offended.'

'I don't intend any offence to the Prince, it's you I'm thinking about. You're just a girl. I'd never forgive myself if I exploited you,' he told her. *Well, actually I could*, he admitted to himself, *but I have to at least make a damned good effort to do the right thing*.

'Exploited?' she repeated, with the merest suggestion of a frown.

'I'd be *using* you. Taking advantage of you because the Prince has asked you to come to me.'

'He didn't ask me, he ordered me,' she said, 'and if I don't obey his orders he will have me beaten.'

'He will?' asked Travis, rather surprised. He hadn't thought of Prince Valerie as that sort of person.

She turned and showed him her back. He could make out traces of fading welts criss-crossing her back. She turned to face him again. 'See?'

'Well, that changes everything,' he said, secretly relieved. 'We can't have that happening to you again.'

'Good,' she said, and smiled for the first time. It was only a faint smile but it was definitely a smile.

'What's your name?' he asked.

'Annabelle,' she said then walked over to him and kissed him on the mouth. Her lips were cool. She helped him out of his gown and led him over to the bed.

He had feared, from her quiet, passive manner, that her love-making would relate to that of an unresponsive lump of meat, albeit a beautifully upholstered lump of meat, but as soon as they were on the bed she surprised him pleasantly by immediately becoming extremely animated and very passionate. And inventive. Who ever had tutored her must have had an honours degree in the art of sexual arousal. And to his relief, she seemed to be getting as much enjoyment out of their activities as he was. He didn't think she was a good enough actress to fake it so enthusiastically. This served to extinguish completely any remaining feelings of guilt.

As he made love to her a second time, this time penetrating her from behind – at her suggestion – it occurred to him that the Prince had sent her to him as a way of taking his mind off Beatrice. A kind of consolation prize. He should have been annoyed that the Prince regarded him as so shallow a person, but right then and there he didn't give a damn.

Later, as they lay exhausted side by side, he raised himself on one elbow and stared at her. 'You're very beautiful, Annabelle.'

'Thank you, sir, but I think my nose is too big, and my breasts are too small.'

'No, no, they're *fine*, believe me. But tell me, do you always wear that ribbon when you make love. Not that I'm complaining, mind. I think it's sort of kinky.'

'Kinky?'

'Sexy.'

'Oh. No, I wear it because the Prince asks me to.'

It was Travis's turn to say, 'Oh.' His curiosity had become aroused.

When she fell into a deep sleep, her arms around him, he very slowly undid the ribbon.

Even in the dim, flickering candlelight the two neat punctures in the side of her throat were clearly visible.

He had seen more than enough Hammer horror films to realize their significance.

Chapter Eleven

Travis broke out in a cold sweat. The implications were clear. The two holes in her neck meant that there was a vampire in the vicinity, and for some reason he felt sure that it was none other than Prince Valerie himself. Then something else occured to him – what if Annabelle was a vampire as well?

Was he sharing a bed with a *vampire*?

He carefully retied the ribbon around her neck and then gently pushed up a corner of her top lip until he could see her teeth. No fangs were visible, just ordinary teeth. But then maybe she had retractable fangs . . .

She started to stir and Travis jerked his hand away from her mouth. She opened her eyes. 'What were you doing?'

'Oh, nothing.'

She sat up. 'You were doing something to my mouth.'

'I was just looking at your teeth.'

'Why?'

'I'm fascinated by other people's teeth. Can never resist checking them out.'

'You're strange.'

You can talk, he thought.

'But you're very nice,' she added and leaned over to kiss him. He flinched away from her lips.

She frowned. 'What's the matter?'

'Admit it, you were going to bite me,' he said.

'Bite you? Why would I want to bite you?'

Be careful, he told himself. He couldn't let on that he suspected she was a vampire. She would be sure to tell Prince Valerie and there was a fair chance that the Prince might not like the news that he was a blood-sucker to be spread around. Then again, perhaps the Prince had sent Annabelle to Travis in order to turn *him* into a vampire . . .

She suddenly rolled on top of him, pinning him to the bed. 'Arghhh,' he said, he knew it would be useless to resist. It was common knowledge that vampires had the strength of ten men. In this case it would be ten women, but that was still more than sufficient to subdue him.

'What's wrong with you all of a sudden?' she asked, 'What's got into you?'

'It's what's got into *you* that I'm worried about,' he said, making the sign of the cross with his fingers in front of her face. She went cross-eyed as she stared, mystified, at his two forefingers.

'I don't understand,' she said.

'Neither do I,' said another voice, 'but don't let that stop you.'

Travis turned and, to his great relief, saw that Jack had flown in through the narrow window and was sitting on the sill. 'Jack, am I glad to see you!' he cried.

'You are?' asked Jack, sounding surprised.

Travis pushed Annabelle over onto her side and leapt out of the bed. 'Jack, this is Annabelle. She's just leaving.'

'I am?' she asked, echoing Jack's surprised tone.

'Indeed,' he said and gave her her gown.'Thanks, it's been marvellous.' As she got out of the bed he took her hand and shook it. 'Goodbye. See you round the castle, no doubt.'

She put on her robe, gave him another mystified look, picked up her candle and left.

'Alright, I admit it' said Jack, 'you've got me stymied. Is there a good reason why you just kicked that foxy-looking babe out of bed?'

'She might be a vampire,' said Travis as he collapsed back down on the bed.

'So? Nobody's perfect.'

'I'm serious,' he said and told Jack about the bite marks he'd found on her neck under the ribbon.

'Oh, that explains that business with the fingers. You were trying to make a cross, eh?'

'Yes, but it didn't seem to have any effect on her.'

'Well, it wouldn't, would it dickwit? Think about it.'

'What do you mean?'

'You seen any churches around here since you arrived?'

Travis thought about it. 'No,' he said.

'That's because Christianity is thin on the ground in this world. There isn't any. Oy vey, did *you* have the wrong vampire, as they said in a movie I saw once. But you don't know she is one for sure.'

Travis rubbed his chin. 'No, but I'd bet the Prince is.'

'I told you there was something fishy about the guy,' said Jack, triumphantly.

'And yet,' said Travis, 'he was walking around in broad daylight earlier.'

'Maybe he was wearing a strong sun-block,' said Jack. 'Look, Travis, even if vampires do exist here, and I've heard rumours that they do, it doesn't mean they have to obey the same rules as our home-grown variety. Besides, all that stuff was made up by writers. Like that Brad Stoker guy. They aren't laws set in stone. Hell, in my movie *The Night of the Nympho-Vampires*, our vampire babes could only be killed with silver-plated vibrators. I made that rule up all by myself.'

'I'm sure you did.'

'The point is, dickwit, that if there *are* real vampires here, a whole different set of rules probably applies to them.'

'Yes, you're right,' said Travis. 'And I have to find out what they are if I'm going to help Beatrice.'

'What's the royal babe got to do with it?'

'It's obvious! She's clearly besotted with Valerie and in the carriage earlier he admitted he was looking for a wife. If I don't do something she'll end up the bride of a vampire!'

'*Bride of a Vampire*, eh? That brings back more memories. I made a movie with that very title back in '82. Brought it in for under two hundred thousand dollars and grossed nearly three million. Starred Mixie O'Connor.' Jack sighed at the memory. 'Great little broad. Enormous bazooms and went off like a Turk's fart between the sheets. One time she . . .'

'Excuse me,' interrupted Travis. 'Your career in movies is all very fascinating, if incredibly disgusting, but can we return to the matter in hand. How can I save Beatrice from a fate worse than death?'

'More like a fate worse than life.'

'I've got to warn her somehow.'

'But first you've got to find out whether Prince Val really is a vampire,' Jack pointed out.

Travis sat down heavily on the bed. 'Yes. But how, if vampires operate under different rules here?'

'Process of elimination,' said Jack. 'First check out all the traditional rules from the stories back on Earth. You never know, some may still apply here.'

Travis brightened. 'Great idea. I'll do it!'

'Do you like garlic?' Travis asked Prince Valerie.

The Prince raised an eyebrow. 'What is garlic?'

'Oh, a herb.Maybe you don't have it here. It's popular in my world. Well, with some people . . .' *Scratch the garlic*, Travis told himself. He wasn't having much luck so far at establishing the Prince's possible vampirific tendencies. At the start of breakfast Travis had made a show of admiring a silver plate, holding it in such a way that he caught the Prince's reflection in it. And the Prince definitely *had* a reflection, so that old Earth rule about vampires certainly didn't apply here. Also he ate normal food and drank wine which further separated him from the vampires of Earth folklore. Travis was running out of ideas. Short of leaping on the Prince and hammering a wooden stake through his heart – which was a bit drastic and would be awfully embarrassing if it turned out that the Prince wasn't a vampire after all – he couldn't think of a sure-fire way to find out the truth. Perhaps Annabelle simply had a lover with unusually long incisors who got too enthusiastic when it came to love-bites.

Breakfast was a more intimate affair than the previous night's dinner. Apart from the Prince, Beatrice, Damion and himself there were only a few courtiers present and they all sat around a single table in the dining hall. When the Prince and Beatrice had arrived Travis was relieved to see she wasn't wearing a tell-tale ribbon around her neck. Even so, he had stared hard at her neck and throat for any sign, no matter how small, of forced entry.

'Hello Travis,' she had greeted him as she sat down. 'Why are you showing such intense interest in my neck?'

Though pleased that she'd at least acknowledged his existence today, her question had caught him off-guard. Glancing anxiously at the Prince, who was also regarding him with a quizzical expression, Travis had said quickly, 'Your neck? No, no, I wasn't staring at your neck . . .'

'Well, it certainly seemed so to me,' replied Beatrice, who was wearing another low-cut number, this time in emerald green. 'If it wasn't my neck, what *were* you staring at?' And she glanced down at her bosom with a playful smile.

It might have been a game to her, but to Travis all this talk of necks in front of the Prince was far from amusing. Just the bloody opposite. He had to change the subject, fast.

'Er, sleep well, Princess?' he asked.

'I had a wonderful night,' she told him.

What the hell did *that* mean? Was she still a virgin, he wondered worriedly. Was that a post-coital flush he spied on her exquisite cheeks? Ascertaining the state of her virginity was going to take a lot more work than a close look at her neck.

'Damion tells me you are going to give us a demonstration of your marvellous talisman after breakfast,' the Prince said as he deftly deconstructed a roast chicken.

'Yes, I am,' said Travis. He felt uncomfortable without the gun and hoped that Damion would let him keep it after the demonstration. Somehow he doubted it.

Damion, who was sitting beside him, said, 'It's a most intriguing device. I spent hours examining it, but all my efforts to dismantle it were in vain.'

Thank goodness for that, thought Travis.

'It's a mechanical device, you say, yet there is a powerful magical aura surrounding it,' said Damion.

'In my world it would be just a mechanical device but here it's different.'

'Does everyone possess one of these devices in your world?' Damion asked.

'Well, in my country they're hard to come by if you're just an ordinary citizen. There's a country called the United States of America, though, where everyone owns at least two or three of the damned things. Gun ownership there seems to be compulsory by law, and shooting at each other is the major national pastime.'

'They are used in warfare between kingdoms too?' the Prince asked him.

'Oh yes. And they get much bigger than the one I have. They're called rifles, machine guns, artillery . . . the slaughter they cause is incredible.' Travis smiled sourly. 'We're very good at mass slaughter.'

'I look forward to the demonstration,' said the Prince, exchanging a glance with Damion. 'But tell me, was the servant, Annabelle, that I put at your service, satisfactory?'

He could feel himself blushing. 'Perfectly satisfactory, Your Highness,' Travis said.

'She tended your every . . . need?'

'Oh, yes! She did indeed. Excellent little worker. Any time she wants a reference just let me know,' he said and grabbed frantically at a tankard of beer from which he gulped down several mouthfuls. He was aware of Beatrice's eyes upon him.

'And what "needs" did this Annabelle tend for you, Travis?' she enquired sweetly.

'Oh, you know, the usual servanty things.'

'Like what?'

'Oh, she ran me a bath, laid out my clothes, helped me dress . . . and so on.'

'It's the "so on" that interests me,' said Beatrice.

He was saved by the Prince who said, 'You're embarrassing our guest, my darling. Why don't you tell him our good news?'

Travis waited apprehensively. The double use of the word *our* bothered him.

'Prince Valerie is holding a ball in my honour tonight.

You're invited, of course. And the Prince will be making an important announcement. About us.'

He groaned inwardly. He knew what was coming.

She gave the Prince an adoring look then turned back to Travis and said happily, 'He has asked me to marry him and I've accepted.'

Travis forced a beaming smile at them both and said, 'Congratulations. I hope you'll be very happy.'

Shit, shit, shit, he said under his breath.

Travis aimed at the archery target set up at the far end of a small courtyard and fired several times. The boom of the gun echoed back and forth around the thick stone walls. He also heard the bullets strike the masonry after passing straight through the straw target.

'A dangerous power indeed,' said the Prince.

'May I?' asked Damion, extending his hand.

Reluctantly, Travis gave him back the automatic. Damion aimed at the target. 'All I have to do is pull on this little lever, correct?' he asked.

'Yes. It's called a trigger.'

He waited expectantly, but though he saw Damion's knuckle whiten from the effort to pull the trigger, nothing happened.

'It won't work,' said Damion.

'Let me see.' Travis took the gun and checked it. The safety catch wasn't on so it should have gone off. He aimed at the target and pulled the trigger. The gun fired. He gave it back to Damion. 'Try again.'

Damion did so, but the gun still refused to fire for him. The Prince then took the gun and tried to shoot it. Nothing happened. 'Curious,' said Damion. 'It seems that it only works for you.'

Surprised, Travis nodded.

'Is that how these weapons operate in your world?' Damion asked. 'They can only be used by their owners?'

'No, I guess this is part of the magical aspect to this particular gun. To be honest, I didn't know about this before.'

'As a mere mechanical device, do you know how it functions?' asked Damion.

'I know the basics, more or less.'

'Could you draw a diagram of the mechanism?' asked Damion.

'Yes, I think so.'

'Good,' said Damion. He and the Prince then walked over to the target to examine the damage more closely. Travis seized his chance. He leaned close to Beatrice and whispered, 'Beatrice, you can't marry Prince Valerie!'

'Why ever not?'

'Because he's a vampire!'

'I beg your pardon?'

'Well, I can't prove it exactly but, I'm pretty certain he *is* one.'

'A vampire? Have you fallen off your horse and hit your head again?' asked Beatrice.

'No, I haven't! You must believe me! The servant girl that the Prince sent to sleep with me last night – Annabelle – had teeth marks in her neck! Deep ones!'

'So you *did* sleep with her. I thought so.'

'Will you listen to me?' he cried, grabbing her arm, 'Someone has been using her as a human drinks' cabinet and the prime suspect has to be her master, the Prince. And if you're not careful you'll end up the same. Or even worse, he might turn you into a vampire as well!'

'You're talking nonsense. Because you're jealous.'

'I am not! Talking nonsense, I mean. You don't want to be a vampire, believe me! You'll have to sleep in a coffin full of dirt. Think of the laundry bills alone!'

The Prince and Damion were returning. Travis let go of her. 'If you don't believe me check him out yourself!' he whispered fiercely.

'And what are you two talking about so intensely?' asked the Prince as he approached.

'Oh, nothing in particular,' said Travis, 'just social chit-chat.'

'Travis told me he thinks you're a vampire,' Beatrice said, with a smile.

Chapter Twelve

'She actually told him that?' asked Jack.

'Yes. She told him I thought he was a vampire.'

'And how did he take it?'

'He laughed it off. Or rather, I think he pretended to. I have no idea how he really feels about it. Not too happy, I would guess. *Damn* . . .'

'What are you doing there?' Jack flew down from the rafter he'd been sitting on and landed on the table in front of Travis. He peered at the sheet of coarse paper that Travis was drawing on with a quill pen. 'What's that supposed to be?'

'What does it look like?'

'A prehistoric dildo.'

'It's a gun, you idiot. I'm trying to do a diagram of the Colt .45 for Damion.'

'Why?'

'I think he and the Prince intend to become arms manufacturers,' he said, and told Jack of the interest in guns displayed by the pair. 'I thought I knew how a gun worked but now I realize I don't. I mean, I know the basics but haven't a clue about the details.'

'Just make something up,' suggested Jack, 'it won't matter. They haven't a hope of trying to build a gun here, even if you gave them an accurate diagram. They don't have the tools. And they haven't invented gunpowder yet.'

'I hope you're right. And I didn't like the idea of being responsible for introducing guns to this world.' He leaned back in his seat and sighed. 'Fortunately Damion can't use my gun,' he said, describing how the Colt refused to function for either Damion or the Prince. 'I wish I could get the gun back from Damion. I feel so damned vulnerable without it.'

'I might be able to help you out there,' said Jack, flying back to his perch on the rafter.

'How?'

'I've been doing a fair amount of exploring in this joint. On the sly, of course. I know where the little jerk's laboratory or workshop or whatever he calls it is located. In fact I had an interesting encounter with a cute little succubus he keeps locked up in there. I'd tell you what we did together but I know how easily shocked you are . . .'

'I appreciate that,' said Travis. 'You think that's where he keeps my gun?'

'It's likely. I'll give the place a thorough search tonight. After I finish my business with Sharon, natch.' He grinned evilly.

'Sharon?'

'The succubus. That's her name.'

'A succubus called *Sharon*?'

'Sure. What's wrong with that?'

'Nothing. She doesn't have a sister called Tracy, does she?'

'No. I think she said she had a sister called Cheryl. Why?'

'Forget it. Look, I'll slip away from the ball tonight and come and help you search Damion's place, if you'll give me directions.'

'Sure.'

'And don't worry, I'll make sure that I arrive after you and er, Sharon have finished whatever disgusting things you get up to.'

Jack chuckled. 'You'll miss the experience of a lifetime.'

Travis shuddered.

Later that day, while Travis was lying on his bed trying to come up with a foolproof strategy to convince Beatrice that her future husband was probably severely dysfunctional – i.e. one of the living dead – there came a knock on the door. He called 'Come in!' Annabelle entered carrying a large box made of crude cardboard. Travis nervously got up off the bed. 'Oh, hello Annabelle,' he said with forced cheerfulness.

'Your costume for the ball tonight, sir,' she said sullenly. As she put the box down on the bed he noticed she moved stiffly as if in pain. He also saw that her face was drawn and her eyes were puffy.

'Costume?'

'It's a costume ball, sir,' she told him.

'But we're already wearing costumes . . .' He stopped, realizing she wouldn't understand what he meant. As she turned to leave he saw streaks of red seeping through the back of her dress. 'Wait,' he said. She turned to face him again. 'Yes, sir?'

'Annabelle, what happened to you? Were you beaten again?'

'My Master had me whipped,' she told him blankly.

'But why?' asked Travis, shocked. 'You obeyed him in every way last night.'

'It wasn't because of what we did together. It was because he thinks I betrayed him. By telling you his secret.'

Then he is a vampire! thought Travis excitedly. 'But you didn't tell me anything!'

She nodded. 'He knows I would never have told you outright but you must have learnt of his vampirism through some act of carelessness of mine. Which you clearly did.'

'It wasn't your fault. When you were asleep I undid your ribbon. I saw the puncture marks in your neck.'

'I shouldn't have fallen asleep.'

'It still wasn't your fault. The ribbon intrigued me. And when you said you wore it because of the Prince's wishes . . . well, I couldn't resist untying it.'

'That was why you started acting strangely when I woke up. You thought I was a vampire too!'

Travis gave a nervous laugh. 'Don't take this personally, but *are* you one?'

'No. The Prince takes care not to infect me with the curse.'

'I see,' said Travis, deciding he would have to give her the benefit of the doubt. 'And how does the Prince feel about me knowing he's a vampire?'

'Apart from being very angry with me he is anxious that you don't spread the information any further.'

Travis thought that sounded ominous. And he was right.

Because then Annabelle said, 'He is not going to let you leave the castle. Alive.'

'Oh,' said Travis, 'you mean he's going to have me killed?'

'Eventually. When he tires of you. But for now he finds you interesting and he thinks you might be of some use to him. He is fascinated by your talisman.'

'I see,' he said. 'But why are you telling me all this?'

'You'll try and escape, won't you?'

'You can bet on it.'

'Then promise me you'll take me with you when you go. I can't stand it here any longer. I hate the Prince.'

That stopped him. How could he promise her such a thing? He was going to have enough trouble escaping himself. And there was Beatrice to consider too . . . 'Look, I'll think about it if you do me a big favour.'

'What's that?'

'Are you in contact at all with the Princess Beatrice?' he asked.

'I haven't been assigned to serve her personally but I could easily go and see her. You want me to give her a message?'

'More than that. I want you to convince her that Prince Valerie is a vampire. Show her your neck or something.'

Annabelle looked very uneasy. 'I don't know . . . if the Prince found out he would have me executed. Very, very slowly.'

'You're already risking your life. I have to save Beatrice from the Prince, silly – ungrateful cow that she is.'

She nodded slowly. 'Very well. I'll try.'

'Thank you,' he said, relieved. Then, 'Look, you know I can't give you any guarantees about our chances of success.'

'Yes, I realize that. But you possess powerful magic. If any one can get the better of the Prince, it's you.'

Travis wished he could agree, but he said nothing, for fear of disillusioning her.

When she had gone he stared out of one of the narrow windows for a time, lost in thought. Then he remembered the box she had brought. Mildly curious, he went over and lifted its lid. He looked inside. *Oh no*. He took the costume out the box and stared at it. There was no way of avoiding the awful truth: he was going to the ball dressed as a giant white rabbit!

'It suits you,' said Jack.

'No, really, tell me honestly,' pleaded Travis, his voice muffled by the rabbit head.

'It *really* suits you. You look stupid.'

'I thought so.' He removed the head and examined it again. One of the ears drooped in a silly-looking fashion. The entire head was silly-looking. Come to that, the entire *costume* was silly-looking. Someone had it in for him, and he had a damn good idea who that someone was.

He sighed and said, 'I'll give you about an hour after the start of the ball and then I'll sneak away and join you in Damion's workshop.'

'Okay. You sure you know how to find it?'

'I've memorized your directions. I'd suggest we synchronize our watches, if there were such things as watches here.'

'Try not to come too early unless you wanna see me and Sharon in action.'

'Don't worry, I don't.' He looked doubtfully at the rabbit head again. 'Well, I suppose I'd better get going. At least, with this animal theme running through all the ball costumes, I won't be the only stupid-looking one there.'

Wrong again. He *was* the only stupid-looking one there. True, an animal motif ran through all the costumes, but it only applied to the masks and other headgear. The remainder of the outfits consisted of brightly-coloured tunics and tights for the men and lavish gowns for the women. Travis was the sole guest wearing a full-body animal suit. To make things even worse, the construction of the lower half meant that he had to move by making a series of little hops. Very soon he was attracting a great deal of attention and became the source of much merriment. He cursed Prince Valerie.

It also proved to be a very uncomfortable suit to wear – it was hot and sticky inside – and the head was a real nuisance. It was difficult to see through the eyeholes and the mouth would hardly open. He tried having a drink of beer and only succeeded in pouring the liquid down his front. Eating was completely out of the question. He would have to wait for the official unmasking at midnight, and by that time he was sure that all the food would be gone.

Travis was trying to find Beatrice but the damned masks, not to mention the fact that he could hardly see through his own, had so far rendered that an impossible task. He'd already made a couple of blunders, approaching or rather hopping up to, women he thought might be her and loudly whispering, 'Beatrice? It's me, Travis!' in their mystified ears. There were lots of male and female servants around, serving drinks and food, but they too wore masks and if Annabelle was among them it was equally impossible to tell. He felt increasingly frustrated: he was dying to know whether Annabelle had succeeded in reaching Beatrice and convincing her that Prince Val, her husband-to-be, was a no-good, blood-sucking, servant-beating, son-of-a-bitch, stinking vampire. Or words to that effect. Then there was the worrying possibility that Annabelle had tried to tell Beatrice about Val and she hadn't believed the girl. What if she had immediately blabbed to Val what Annabelle had told her? If that was the case then the game was up. After some 'pressure' from the Prince, Annabelle would have surely confessed everything, including Travis's intention to escape. And he didn't like to think about what might have happened to Annabelle after that.

He hopped around in an aimless fashion, trying to ignore the pointed fingers and the sniggers and wondering how much time had passed since his arrival in the Great Hall. He was thinking about making another attempt at drinking something when suddenly a large bulk of a man swam into his limited field of vision. The man wore the mask of a bear's face and his massive body was concealed in a voluminous cloak.

'Having a good time, Travis?' rumbled a deep voice with an odd accent to it that he vaguely recognized.

'Far from it, matey . . . hey, you know my name! Have we met before?'

'Yes. Just the once. It was a fateful encounter. Certainly a fateful one for you.'

'Here at the castle?' asked Travis, trying to remember meeting anyone this large among the Prince's entourage. So far the only encounter he'd had here that was even remotely fateful was the one with Annabelle.

'No, not here,' said the man. His eyes appeared to glow behind the mask. 'Where we met was a long way from here. A *very* long way.'

Travis's blood ran cold, then hot. Then cold again. He felt both terrified and excited. Anxious and hopeful. He knew who this man was now.

It was Prenderghast. Gideon Leonard *Prenderghast.*

Chapter Thirteen

'It's over, is it?' Travis asked hopefully.

'What is?' asked the man who Travis knew was Prenderghast.

Travis spread his paws. 'All this. This . . . this . . . *charade* of yours. I knew all along it wasn't real.'

'Oh, it's real okay, Travis. Believe me,' rumbled Prenderghast. 'And I hope you appreciate the time and effort it took me to find this tailor-made world for you and your arrogant preconceptions. I had to do a lot of searching through the infinite Variations of Existence.'

One of us is definitely mad, thought Travis, *and I certainly hope it's not me.* 'Well, don't think I don't appreciate it, sir,' he said, deciding it would be best to humour his tormentor. 'It's been a real learning experience but I'd like to go home now. If you don't mind.'

'You can't go home yet, Travis. You know the rules. You may *never* make it home again unless you find the Key.'

Travis was getting a definite sinking feeling. 'Oh yes, the key. Sorry . . . the Key. I forgot. Okay, so how about giving me a clue as to where it is? And *what* it is.'

The bear mask shook from side to side. 'No. I can't do that. All I can do is repeat what Jack has already told you – that you'll recognize it when you see it.'

'That's a bloody lot of good.'

'Best I can do, Travis. But I do have this for you.' He reached into his cloak and produced a brown paper parcel. He extended it to Travis who took it eagerly. He'd been hoping it contained another gun but was disappointed when he felt how light the parcel was. Prenderghast then abruptly turned and began to walk away.

'Wait!' cried Travis. 'Don't go!'

'Have to,' rumbled Prenderghast over his shoulder, 'People to see, things to do.'

And the next moment Prenderghast was swallowed up by the surrounding crowd. Travis charged after him. 'Wait!' he cried. 'Don't leave me here! I'm sorry for what I said to you back in your office . . .' He pushed people aside but there was no sign of Prenderghast. Then he stepped on something that crumbled under his foot. He looked down, with difficulty. The ruined bear mask stared back up at him with empty eyes from the floor. He knew at once he wouldn't find Prenderghast in the Great Hall, or anywhere else in the castle. He had gone.

Travis muttered *shit*. Then he remembered the parcel he was still holding. He tore, or rather pawed, off the brown paper. Then he said *shit* again, which was rather appropriate considering what he found himself staring at.

A double pack of toilet rolls

Travis knocked tentatively on the big wooden door. It swung open slightly. He pushed it further until he could slip through. 'Jack?' he whispered, as he looked around and waited for his eyes to adjust to the gloom. He had taken off the damned rabbit's head and was holding it under his arms, along with the toilet rolls.

'Right here, boss,' said the demon as he landed on his shoulder. 'What do you think of this joint?'

'It's sure big,' said Travis. Which was true. Damion's little workshop turned out to be a dungeon of cavernous proportions. Strange objects lay scattered about, they mostly appeared to be instruments of torture. *Things* suspended from chains hung from the vaulted ceiling. He stopped trying to adjust his eyes in case he saw too clearly what they were. The walls were lined with shelves that held rows of bottles and many large glass jars in which floated more *things*. The place was festooned with the mandatory spider webs, complete with fat, hairy spiders, and bats flittered about overhead. And as a finishing touch, greenish slime oozed from the walls and ceiling. 'I'd hate to meet his interior decorator on a dark night,' said Travis.

'I think that's the guy over there,' said Jack, pointing at

one of the large jars. 'Come on, I'll introduce you to Sharon . . .' He took off from Travis's shoulder.

'I can't wait,' muttered Travis as he followed Jack into the unhealthy depths of Damion's playpen.

'You wow them at the ball with your rabbit act, Bugs?' asked Jack.

'Not exactly. And you'll be interested to know that there was an unexpected guest there. Very unexpected.'

'Who?'

'I'll tell you later . . . arghh . . .' Travis had walked into a large spider web that seemed to have the tensile strength of carbon fibre. He tried to back away from it but suddenly realized he was stuck to it. Then, out of the corner of his eye, he saw something moving towards him across the web. It was the biggest spider he'd ever seen. 'Oh Jack,' he called, 'I have a problem here!'

The insect picked up speed. Travis threw the rabbit's head at it, which slowed it up but not by much. 'JACK!'

Jack swooped down and spat fire at the scuttling spider, scoring a direct hit. The spider made a high-pitched squealing sound and fell, burning, from the web. It hit the floor and curled up in a smouldering ball. It was, Travis estimated, the size of a dinner plate. 'Thanks,' he told Jack and tried to pull himself free of the web.

'You think I could stand by and watch a defenceless rabbit become spider food?' he said as he began to help Travis extricate himself from the sticky web. It took a lot of effort before they succeeded, and when they did, the web was covered with fake rabbit fur. He picked up the head, and the packet of toilet rolls which he'd dropped during the struggle. He heard Jack whistle in surprise.

'Where'd you get *those*?' he asked.

'I found a branch of 7-Eleven behind the stables.'

'No, seriously!'

'It's to do with that unexpected guest I mentioned. I'll explain it all later. Is it much further?'

'Not far.'

Travis followed Jack around a large pillar and saw, in the flickering light of a torch on the wall, Sharon.

He wasn't sure what he'd been expecting. Something like Jack, he guessed, only female. But she wasn't anything like Jack. For one thing, she wasn't small like Jack, she was human-sized. Nor was she an ugly-looking monster. On the contrary, she was exquisite.

She was reclining on her elbows across the top of a large desk and she was quite, quite naked. Travis had never seen a naked woman who looked as totally naked as she did. She had shiny brown skin, shiny black hair, shiny green eyes and pointed ears. Then he noticed that she wasn't completely naked – there was a metal band around her left ankle, and attached to it was a thin chain that disappeared beneath the desk.

Landing on his shoulder again, Jack said, 'Travis, meet Sharon. Sharon, say hello to Travis.'

She raised a limp hand in greeting and said, 'Hello, Travis.'

He cleared his throat. 'Er, hello, Sharon. Pleased to meet you.'

Jack said proudly, 'So what do you think of her?'

'I'm impressed . . . if rather surprised.'

'Why?'

Travis hesitated, but if Sharon resented being talked about as if she wasn't there she gave no sign, so he said, 'Well, I thought a succubus was a demon.'

'They are. She is.'

'But she doesn't look very demonic.'

'Look, Bugs, her main job is to seduce mortal men. She could hardly do that if she looked like me, now could she?'

'You have a point. But there's something else. The difference between you two . . .'

'The age difference you mean? Nah, that's not a problem.'

'I meant her size.'

'What's wrong with her size?' demanded Jack.

'Nothing. She's perfect. But you said that you and she were, well, getting it on.'

'We sure are. Ain't we babe?'

She stuck her tongue out at Jack. It was pink and pointed. A shiver ran through Travis. 'But you being so . . . your size, and she being her size, how do you manage it?'

'Want to see?' asked Jack.

'I don't think I want a demonstration. Thanks anyway.'

'That's not what I meant. Sharon, show him your party trick!'

'Sure, hon,' said Sharon and closed her eyes. To Travis's surprise, she began to shrink. Slowly at first, and then faster. Within about thirty seconds she was the same size as Jack. Jack flew over and landed on the table beside her. 'Pretty fancy, eh Bugs?'

'Very. But if she can do that, why doesn't she simply slip off the . . .' Then he saw that the manacle around her ankle had shrunk too. 'Magic, huh?' he said.

'Magic,' agreed Jack.

'Why does Damion keep her prisoner?' asked Travis.

'Why do you think? To screw her, of course.'

'Oh . . .' said Travis, embarrassed.

'It's not just the sex,' said Jack. 'Explain to him, babe.'

'By having me before he performs some act of sorcery he increases his power,' said Sharon. Her voice was low and husky. Another shiver ran through Travis.

'Our Damion may look like a kid but he's a master of the dark arts,' said Jack, producing his inevitable pack of Marlboro. 'And dangerous.'

'They make a fine couple, him and his vampire master,' muttered Travis.

'So you're going to help Sharon here, Bugs?' Jack patted the miniature Sharon on one of her shiny thighs.

'Help her do what?'

'Escape, of course. She wants to get out of Damion's sleazy clutches. She may be a succubus but she does have her standards.'

'How can I do that?'

'I have a hunch that your magic Colt will be able to break this frigging chain,' said Jack.

'Really?' Travis went to the desk and lifted a section of chain. It felt light and flimsy but it also made his fingers tingle as if an electrical charge was running through it. 'Well, fine, I'm willing to have a go, but first we have to find the Colt. Have you had a chance to search for it yet?'

'Yeah, I got started. No luck so far but it's here somewhere. I can feel it.'

'Well, as soon as we find it I'll try it on the chain. If it works, Sharon can be on her merry, if demonic, way.'

'Uh-uh,' said Jack. 'She'll be coming with us.'

'What?' asked Travis, knowing he wasn't going to like what he was about to hear.

Jack put an arm around Sharon's shoulder. 'We're an item, Bugs. We want to stay together.'

'Good grief.' This was all he needed. First Annabelle and now her. By the time they got around to making their escape attempt they would have half the castle's population tagging along. It would make *The Great Escape* look like a minor production.

'Please say yes,' pleaded Sharon, in her excitingly husky voice. Then she started to grow. In seconds she was back to full size. 'I'd be very grateful.'

Travis looked away. 'Let's find that damned gun,' he said nervously.

During the next hour or so Travis found a lot of strange and unusual items in Damion's dubious workshop, most of which he wished he hadn't, but he couldn't find the gun. Nor could Jack. Travis walked over to Jack's side, where the demon was rummaging through a large chest. It appeared to be full of skulls. 'I'm going to have to leave. It'll be time for the unmasking soon, and then I'll be able to find Beatrice. You keep looking. If you find it, bring it to me. But as surreptitiously as possible.'

'Sure thing, Bugs. Hop to it.'

Soon afterwards Travis was back in the Great Hall and back inside the suffocating rabbit's head. He was still incredibly thirsty, but a servant girl – not Annabelle, unfortunately – informed him that midnight was only minutes away. A short time later a gong was rung several times and a herald announced that the unmasking was to begin. Two people, hand in hand, mounted a dais at the end of the Hall. A man and a woman. The man wore the mask of a stag, complete with antlers. The woman wore a deer's head. They turned and faced the mass of revellers. As one they removed their masks. By then Travis wasn't surprised to see that the couple were Prince Valerie and Beatrice. The Prince looked smug and happy, Beatrice looked radiant. She didn't look like a woman who has just been informed that her husband-to-be suffered from a serious drinking problem.

At a signal from the Prince, everyone else began to remove their headgear. With relief, Travis tore off the dreaded rabbit's head and tossed it away. He anxiously scanned the crowd, looking for Annabelle among the servant girls. He couldn't see her, which increased his anxiety . . . But he did notice a man who hadn't removed his mask. He noticed him because he was heading straight towards him. For a brief moment he hoped it might be Prenderghast again but no, this man was too slender. And the mask he wore was that of a bird of prey. And as the man grew closer Travis also noticed that he walked with a pronounced limp.

Travis waited with mounting curiosity as the stranger pushed his way through the crowd and stood directly in front of him. The man removed the bird mask with a flourish.

Travis forced a smile. 'Well, hi there, Sir Rodney! How's the foot?'

Chapter Fourteen

Sir Rodney drew his rapier and pointed it at Travis's throat. 'Prepare to die, you treacherous dog!' he hissed.

'Actually, I'm supposed to be a rabbit,' Travis told him, wishing he had his own rapier with him, but with this ridiculous costume it had been out of the question.

'You can joke all you want, wizard, but you're still going to die. Now on your knees and beg that I end your miserable life swiftly!'

'I prefer to beg from a standing position,' said Travis, aware that their confrontation was beginning to attract attention. A circle of on-lookers was forming around them. 'But before you start getting carried away, Prince Valerie might not like you spilling blood on his big night. And by the way, he intends to marry Beatrice.'

'I will deal with him later,' said Sir Rodney, 'but your death is my burning priority.'

'As a mere commoner I'm flattered,' said Travis, glancing around in the hope of seeing some form of cavalry approaching. And yes, someone of authority was entering the circle, but it wasn't the cavalry, it was Damion. *Oh well,* thought Travis, any little fart in a storm.

'What occurs here?' demanded Damion. He turned to Sir Rodney. 'Who are you?'

'I am Sir Rodney Swash, knight of the kingdom of Vallium and loyal subject of King Morbia.'

'Can I see your invitation?' asked Damion.

'I'm afraid I don't have one. You must forgive my intrusion, sir, but I had to confront this evil wizard and exact my revenge,' said Sir Rodney.

'He's no wizard,' said Damion, 'and I should know because I *am* a wizard . . .'

'He's a wizard in my book, sir. He used magic to bewitch

my beloved away from me. And he used magic to seriously injure me in the foot.' Rodney pointed down at his right boot.

'What's going on here? Who has dared interrupt my festivities?' It was the Prince, closely followed by Beatrice. She looked shocked when she recognized the knight.

'Rodney!' she cried. 'What are you doing here?'

'Princess Beatrice, my beloved!' he cried as he went down on one knee before her. 'I've come to take you home with me!'

'Oh, don't be ridiculous, Rodney,' she told him crossly.

'Who is this dolt?' asked the Prince.

'He's my father's champion knight, so you can imagine the standard of the others. He's suffering from the delusion that we're lovers.' She turned back to Rodney. 'How did you find me so quickly?'

He stood up and said, 'Terry the Tenacious, Vallium's top-ranking barbarian, was a contestant at the convention. He recognized you and immediately returned to Vallium to inform your father . . . and me. So despite the agony I dragged myself from my sick bed and came at once.'

'You needn't have bothered. How's the toe?'

'It was buried with full honours. Your father himself delivered the eulogy at the graveside.'

'I'm sorry about your foot, Rodney,' said Travis, 'but I did try and warn you . . .'

'Save your breath,' Rodney snarled at him. 'It's too late for regrets. You have dishonoured me, not to mention Princess Beatrice, and for that you must die.'

'This is all very entertaining,' said Prince Valerie, 'but where the honour of Princess Beatrice is concerned you must now talk to me. She is soon to be my wife.'

'No, that cannot be!' protested Rodney. 'You must have bewitched her as well.' He turned to Damion. 'Or you! You said yourself you were a wizard.'

'He is,' said Travis quickly. 'He out-bewitched my bewitchery. And ask the Prince about his nocturnal habits. His *drinking* habits, that is.' He knew he wasn't doing himself any favours by saying this but it might be a way of getting Beatrice out of the Prince's clutches.

'The man talks rubbish,' said Damion, scowling at him. 'I did no such thing.'

'He's demented,' added the Prince.

Rodney stood directly in front of the Prince and raised himself to his full height, which meant that the top of his head came up to the Prince's chin. 'Your Highness, I give you fair warning that I mean to take the Princess Beatrice back to Vallium with me.'

The Prince smiled down on him. 'You and whose army?'

'King Morbia's. It is surrounding your castle as we speak.'

'Oh,' said the Prince, clearly taken aback. But he quickly recovered his usual composure, gave Rodney an aloof smile and said, 'What are your terms?'

'You will have twenty-four hours to hand over the Princess,' said Rodney. 'If you fail to comply we will storm the castle, reclaim the Princess, slaughter you all and raze the castle to the ground.'

'Oh, Rodney,' sighed Beatrice, 'trust you to overreact.'

'May I have permission to rejoin my men, your Highness?' Rodney asked the Prince.

'Of course.'

'And may I ask another favour, your highness?'

The Prince gave a slight sigh. 'What is it?'

Rodney pointed at Travis with his sword. 'Your permission to skewer this foul creature right where he stands.'

After only a moment's hesitation the Prince nodded and said, 'Certainly.'

'Valerie, no!' cried Beatrice.

'I'm sorry, my dear, but your former travelling companion is becoming tiresome. I must withdraw my protection from him. Come . . .'

He took Beatrice by the arm and tried to guide her away but she resisted. 'No! You can't let Travis be killed just like that! At least give him a weapon to defend himself with!'

Travis nodded enthusiastically. 'Yes, a weapon would be nice.'

The Prince frowned, then said wearily, 'Oh, very well. Damion, lend him your dagger.'

'Just a dagger?' protested Beatrice. 'That's not fair!'

'It's the only concession I'm prepared to make,' the Prince told her.

Travis raised a paw. 'It's fine with me, sir, but can I ask for one other thing?'

'That depends,' said the Prince, 'on what it is.'

'Can I shuck this damned stupid costume? If I'm to die I want to die like a man, not a rabbit.'

'Very well,' said the Prince.

Travis took his time getting out of the rabbit suit, trying to think of what to do next. He didn't stand a chance against Rodney armed with just a dagger. He could try throwing the thing at him but he didn't think that trick would work twice. Actually, it hadn't even worked the first time . . .

Finally he was out of the costume. Damion held out his dagger to him. Travis took it, then grabbed Damion. He held the dagger against his throat and yelled, 'Okay, Prince, do what I say or your little wizard will end up in one of his own specimen jars!'

There were gasps from the surrounding crowd but the Prince merely smiled at Travis and said, 'What makes you think that I hold the life of Damion in such high regard? I can always get another wizard.'

'Oh, I think you do hold him in high regard, Val old boy. You two have a special relationship. And he knows your little secret, doesn't he? Probably helps you out in the victim department. He knows you're a vampire!'

There were more shocked gasps. The Prince's face darkened with anger. 'You lie!'

Travis dug the tip of the dagger into Damion's throat. Damion gave a little yelp. 'Am I lying, Damion? Come on, speak up.' He dug the dagger a little deeper.

At that point Damion might have confessed, but Travis never found out because just then Rodney, with a yell of 'I've had enough of this!' charged into both Damion and Travis, knocking them flying. On Travis's journey to the floor he lost his hold on the dagger, which also went flying. He landed on his back, hard. He quickly sat up, trying to breathe in. He saw that Rodney had lost his balance after the collision and was on his hands and knees. His rapier lay just in front of him. He was reaching for it. Travis looked around for the dagger. Nowhere to be seen. Rodney had hold of the rapier again . . . was standing . . . preparing to lunge . . .

'Hey, dickwit! Catch!'

Travis looked up. Jack was swooping down. He was carrying the Colt .45. Travis held out his hands. The gun dropped neatly into them. He aimed it at Rodney. Or rather, at Rodney's feet. Rodney stopped his lunge just before it was about to start. He went white. 'Please . . . don't . . .'

Travis stood up. 'Drop your sword,' he ordered Rodney. Rodney obeyed. Travis waved the gun around. 'Everybody freeze!' Nobody moved. Even those who had no idea what Travis was waving in their general direction obviously sensed it was trouble. Jack landed on his shoulder. 'Way to go, dickwit. Tell these bunch of whackos where to get off.'

'Yeah!' cried Travis, flushed with adrenalin. 'Anyone who doesn't toe the line gets it! The boot's on the other foot now, that's for sure!' Then, 'Sorry, Rod, a couple of Freudian slippers there, sport.'

'Dickwit, look out!' yelled Jack.

It was Damion. He had reclaimed his dagger and was about to thrust it into Travis. Travis flung himself to one side, pulling the trigger as he did so. A scream followed the shot. Then more screams as the crowd scattered in all directions. But whoever Travis had hit with the bullet it wasn't Damion. The youthful wizard was still standing and still in possession of his dagger. He lashed out at Travis again but was distracted by Jack who flew straight into his face. Travis brought the barrel of the Colt down hard on Damion's wrist and the dagger fell with a clatter on the stone floor. Damion gave a grunt of pain. Travis looked around. Rodney was lying on the floor and clutching his left foot as he rolled about in agony. 'Not again!' he moaned. There was no sign of either the Prince or Beatrice. Armed guards were pouring into the Great Hall and heading towards Travis. Travis fired at one and he dropped with a scream. The others halted, looking uncertain. Travis pointed the gun at Damion, who was on his knees and holding his right wrist, which looked broken.

'Stand up and tell these goons to back off or I'll make you an ex-wizard. An ex-*everything*!'

His face grey, Damion stood and cried to the guards, 'Stay back! Do as he says!'

To Travis's relief, Damion clearly carried enough weight for the guards to obey him. 'Come on, we're getting out of here.'

'You know where you're going?' asked Jack, fluttering overhead.

'I'm still working on that,' said Travis as he began prodding Damion towards the nearest doorway.

'I know where,' said Jack. 'Back to Damion's place.'

'Are you kidding? We'd be trapped in there!'

'Have faith,' Jack told him.

'Oh, come *on*.'

Travis dropped the heavy bar across the door. With a sneer to his voice Damion said, 'Do you think that will stop the guards for long? They'll batter it down within minutes.'

'Doesn't matter,' called Jack from overhead, 'we have something up our sleeve.'

'We do?' said Travis. Then, quickly, 'Yes, we do.' *I bloody hope so,* he thought. *Trouble is, Jack's not wearing a shirt and I know for a fact there's absolutely nothing up either of my sleeves.* Keeping the barrel of the Colt firmly in the small of the wizard's back, Travis followed Jack into the depths of the dungeon-like room.

'Hi babe,' greeted Jack when they reached Sharon. 'Look what we've brought you.'

Sharon hissed when she saw Damion. He muttered something which sounded to Travis like an incantation. Jack said, as he landed on the table top beside her, 'Don't worry, the little shit has been neutered. Show her the gun, boss.'

Travis obligingly displayed the Colt. 'By the way,' said Travis, 'where did you find it?'

'In a filing cabinet,' Jack told him, 'in a drawer marked "G".'

'All this is useless,' snarled Damion. 'You'll never get out of here alive. And the Prince will make you eat your own innards before he has you killed. And you'll be *happy* to do it!'

Travis raised the gun and tapped him sharply with it on the back of the head. 'Manners,' he said as Damion staggered forward with a cry of pain.

Then began a rhythmic crashing sound. The guards had started work on the door.

Chapter Fifteen

'Quick! Shoot the chain off!' cried Jack. He held up a length of chain, pulled it tight between his hands and turned his head away. Travis aimed the gun carefully and fired. It parted immediately. Both lengths of the chain, including the manacle around Sharon's ankle, began to glow, then everything just turned into glittery dust. Sharon was free. The angry, and very naked, succubus leapt from the table top, ran with a gazelle-like grace over to Damion, who was still staggering around holding his head, and kneed him brutally in the groin. Damion went down making a whooshing sound. Travis almost felt sorry for him. Almost.

The pounding on the distant door continued but so far it was still holding up. Jack said to Sharon, 'Now that you've had your fun let's finish him off and get down to business . . .'

'Happy to oblige, my odious beloved.' Sharon raised her hand, clearly meaning to bring the edge of it down on the back of Damion's exposed neck. 'Wait!' said Travis, springing forward and grabbing her wrist. The look in her eyes made him fear for his own life, then it passed and she said calmly, 'Why did you do that?'

'There are some questions I want to ask him,' Travis told her.

She pulled her arm free from his grip and said, 'I owe you. Do as you please.'

'Oh great,' muttered Jack. 'The bastards will be coming through the door at any moment and you want to play Twenty Questions with the Teenager from Hell.'

'This won't take long,' said Travis. He grabbed Damion by his hair, jerked his head up and stuck the Colt under his nose. 'Listen to me Damion, answer my questions and maybe I won't let Tracy here . . . I mean Sharon, kill you. Understand?'

Damion tried to nod, which was difficult under the circumstances.

'First, is the Prince really a vampire?'

'Yes,' gasped Damion, 'it's a family trait. The Prince's ancestor, Lord Brian the Brazen, made a pact with the King of the Vampires. That's how he established the family's rule over this land, and each male descendant must maintain the pact . . .'

'Hang on a second – aren't vampires supposed to be immortal?' demanded Travis.

Damion managed to look puzzled as well as scared. 'Only the King of the Vampires is immortal, not the ordinary ones,' he said.

'Oh,' said Travis. He decided it was another example of the rules of vampirism differing here. Then he asked, 'And what of Beatrice? What does he have in store for her?'

'He will marry her. And when she has borne him a son she will be offered to the King of the Vampires. It's Clause One of the pact.'

'Bloody hell,' muttered Travis.

'Face it, dickwit,' said Jack, 'that royal babe is natural sacrificial material. Now let's whack pretty boy and get out of here! That door is starting to splinter!'

'Wait! I have one more question!'

'Oh give me a break!' groaned Jack. 'What now? Are you going to ask him his favourite colour?'

Travis ignored him. 'Damion,' he said urgently, 'the servant girl, Annabelle. Do you know what happened to her?'

'Yes. The Prince overheard her trying to talk to the Princess. He . . . questioned her. She is now in the torture chamber. When he has the time he will personally oversee her death.'

Travis said to Jack, 'Do you know where the torture chamber is?'

'Sure.'

'Good.' Travis hit Damion extremely hard on the side of the head with the Colt. He crumpled silently. Travis sincerely hoped he'd killed him. Now he could hear excited voices. The guards had broken through the door at last.

'I presume you know a back way out of here,' he said to Jack. 'Where is it?'

'Right here,' said Jack, pointing to a hole in the bottom of a nearby wall. It was a small hole.

'It's a *drain*!' exclaimed Travis.

'Sure. What did you expect – a revolving door?' He flew down and landed next to the crude drain.

Travis could hear the clatter of approaching armour. 'Er, maybe I'm just being dense but . . .'

'You are being dense,' Jack told him. 'Hand me down the Colt.'

Puzzled, Travis did as he was told.

'Now just take Sharon by the hand, close your eyes and think small.'

The succubus grabbed his hand. It tingled at her touch. He shut his eyes, hoping for a miracle.

'You can look now,' she said in her excitingly husky voice.

He opened his eyes and was immediately disappointed. He was still the same size as her. But then he looked around him and saw that he was also the same size as Jack. He *had*, as he'd hoped he would be, been shrunken by her magic. The furniture, including the table were she had been held prisoner, loomed hugely overhead. And then a very large armoured man galumphed into view, quickly joined by others. The guards were staring about the place, but hadn't spotted them yet.

'Quickly now,' said Jack, throwing the butt of the Colt which hadn't shrunk, back over his shoulder and disappearing into the mouth of the drain.

Travis followed, wondering why they hadn't shrunk the gun as well for the sake of convenience, then remembered it was impervious to the magic of this world. As he entered the drain he almost gagged from the stench but forced himself to keep going. Sharon brought up the rear. At first it was pitch black in the cramped tunnel but then Jack lit one of his cigarettes and the dubious surroundings were illuminated by a dim red glow.

'Can we get to the torture chamber by this route?' he asked Jack.

'After a few deviations in direction, eventually. But are you sure you want to?'

'Yes, it's my fault Annabelle got into trouble. We have to save her if it's not too late. Then we've got to go and rescue Beatrice.'

'Sure. And if we encounter any other damsels in distress we'll liberate them too. I mean, it's not as if we have any other pressing engagements. Like staying alive and getting out of here.'

'You can talk! We've just rescued your precious succubus, haven't we?'

'Hey, watch it,' said Sharon from behind him.

'Sorry. Nothing personal,' Travis told her.

'What I'm trying to point out to you, dickwit, is that the more people we have tagging along after us the harder it's going to be for us to break out of this castle.'

'I'm well aware of that, Jack, but I couldn't live with myself if I didn't at least try and save Beatrice and Annabelle from their horrible fates.'

'For all you know they might just be fictional constructs,' said Jack, scornfully, 'like me and Sharon here.'

'What are you talking about?' asked Sharon.

'Dickwit has this theory that none of us are real,' said Jack.

'That's silly. I *know* I'm real,' protested Sharon.

Feeling her hot breath on the back of his neck, Travis didn't feel inclined to argue. Instead he said to Jack, 'You might be interested to know that I ran into Prenderghast tonight . . .' The next thing he knew he was running into the butt of the Colt because Jack had come to a sudden halt. In turn Sharon ran into the back of him, an altogether more agreeable collision.

'You *what*?!' exclaimed Jack.

Rubbing his nose, Travis said, 'The next time you decide to do that could you bother to give an advance warning?'

'You saw Prenderghast?' asked Jack, peering back at him over his shoulder. 'Where?'

'At the ball. He's the one who gave me the toilet rolls.'

'What's a toilet roll?' asked Sharon.

'It's a roll of soft paper,' Travis told her, 'unless you work in a government building.'

'What's it for?' asked Sharon.

'Well . . .'

'Look, dickwit, you can discuss personal hygiene with her some other time!' cried Jack in exasperation. 'Tell me about Prenderghast! What did he say?'

Travis described his encounter with Prenderghast. Jack gave a sigh when he'd finished.

'So we're still stuck here for the duration,' he muttered.

'Yep. Until I find the Key. Whatever that is.'

Jack started trudging forward again. 'Yeah. Whatever *that* is.'

'What are you two talking about?' asked Sharon.

'Nothing for you to bother your demonic little head about,' Jack told her.

'Patronizing bastard,' she muttered.

Jack came to a sudden halt again. Travis collided with the gun's butt again. 'Ouch! Look, she's right, you *are* a patronizing bastard. Now get moving.'

'Something's coming,' said Jack.

'Something's coming?' cried Travis in disbelief. 'We're in a damned sewer! What could possibly be coming?' Then he blanched and said, 'Oh no, don't tell me it's sewage!'

'No. From the sound of it, it's a very large sewer rat,' replied Jack.

'Oh.'

Jack knelt down.

'What are you doing?'

'Aiming the damned gun, dickwit. I'm going to blow the bloody thing to bits. Get ready to pull the trigger when I say so.'

'Is that necessary? Can't we just scare it away?'

'Listen, I've had encounters with these things before. They don't scare and they're as tough as a female stand-up comic. Now get ready . . . because here it comes! Fire!'

Travis grabbed the trigger with one hand and pulled. It didn't budge.

'I said, *fire*, dickwit!' yelled Jack.

Now Travis could see the approaching rat. From his perspective it looked as big as a tube train but was moving faster. He used both hands on the trigger and pulled again. The trigger moved. And so did he. The recoil sent the Colt hurtling backwards and he was propelled into Sharon. Both were sent flying backwards along the sewer. Not that Travis was fully aware of the situation – the flash and the noise from the detonation had blinded, deafened and generally stunned him.

When he regained part of his senses he realized he was lying on his back on something soft. It felt pleasant, whatever it was.

'Get off me!' the soft, pleasant-feeling something demanded angrily. He rolled of Sharon and shakily stood up. His ears were ringing and his vision blurred. Then he helped Sharon to her feet. He saw Jack climbing over the Colt.

'You guys okay?' asked Jack.

'No,' Travis told him, 'and the next time you have a brilliant idea like that, screw it up and throw it away.'

'Hey, it worked, didn't it? Take a look. The rat is history.'

Travis peered into the gloom ahead. The rat was indeed gone. Or rather, it had been reduced to a series of bloody gobbets of flesh and fur that extended for some distance up the tunnel. He became aware, under the lingering smell of gunpowder, of a stench even worse than the sewer's usual one. 'Oh great. Now we have to walk through all that gunk!'

'Hell, you sure are picky,' said Jack. 'Just hold your nose.' He hefted the Colt over his shoulder and started walking again. Travis reluctantly followed with Sharon again bringing up the rear.

Travis found the next few minutes incredibly unpleasant. Holding his nose helped with the smell, but the squelching sounds his boots made as he stepped on the messy remains of the rat made him want to throw up. He was greatly relieved when they reached the end of the gory trail. 'God that was horrible,' he muttered.

'What was?' asked Sharon. Travis wondered why she sounded as if her mouth was full, then immediately realized, with a shudder, the answer. *Demons*, he thought sourly, *don't you just love 'em?*

After many twists and turns, and what seemed to Travis endless hours of mindless trudging – though thankfully devoid of any further encounters with rats – Jack said, 'We're almost there . . .'

Ahead of Jack and the gun Travis could make out a yellow glow. The drain started up a slight incline and the next thing Travis knew he was following Jack out into a large empty space. Torches glowed far above them on the towering dungeon walls and Travis could hear voices but his view was blocked by a large bed-like structure.

'Let's check out the lay of the land,' said Jack, 'and I'm not referring to you, Sharon. Heh,heh . . .' He quietly put the gun down on the floor and headed off to the nearest corner of the bed-like object. Travis, following, hoped they weren't too late.

Chapter Sixteen

Travis and Jack peered round the corner of the object. Travis saw two muscular, bare-chested and remarkably ugly men seated on stools next to a glowing brazier which held a couple of metal prods and a large pair of crude tongs. Travis didn't need to read their CVs to know what line of business they were in. But where was Annabelle?

One of the thugs scratched a hairy pectoral and mumbled, 'Wish I knew what was keepin' 'im. Not like the Prince to make us wait for a job.'

'Maybe the ball is still going on,' said the other one.

'Nah! Must have been over hours ago. I reckon he isn't going to show, so we might as well get started.'

'Don't be daft! You disobey the Prince and you'll end up on that rack . . .' He pointed towards the object that Travis and Jack were peering round, '. . . and I'll be the poor sod who has to gut you inch by sizzling inch while pulling your spine apart.'

The first one stared at him. 'You'd do it too, wouldn't you? To me, your oldest mate?'

The other shrugged. 'I'd have to. Matter of professional pride. And you'd do the same if it was the other way round.'

The first one considered this, then nodded, 'Yeah, guess I would.'

'Yeah. You're a professional. Like me.'

'Yeah,' said the first one and grinned proudly.

A woman moaned. Travis now knew where Annabelle was. He tapped Jack on the shoulder and signalled. They both hurried back to where Sharon was waiting beside the gun. 'Can you magic me back to my normal size?' he asked her.

'Sure,' she said and extended her hand towards him.

Before he took hold of it he said to Jack, 'When I'm big again bring me the Colt.'

'Sure thing.'

He held Sharon's hand and closed his eyes. Again he felt a tingle in his hand but there was no other sensation. Then he heard her say softly, 'We're there.' He opened his eyes. He was back to his usual size. 'Now you can tell people we grew up together,' said Sharon.

Travis quickly took in the scene. In front of him, stretched out on the rack, was Annabelle. She was dressed in a ragged grey gown which was streaked with blood but she didn't appear to have suffered any serious harm – as far as he could see. She was conscious, and her eyes were widening with surprise as she stared up at Travis and Sharon. As for the two torturers, they too were clearly having trouble coming to terms with what they were seeing. As their eyes popped their jaws dropped. Then they began to rise to their feet.

Jack landed on the side of the rack. 'Here, boss,' handing Travis the gun. Travis aimed at the first torturer and shot him in the forehead. He was sent slamming backwards into the wall, and Travis then shot the other torturer in the side of the head. They ended up lying together on the floor.

'Good shooting,' Jack told him. 'Very professional. I'm sure they would have approved of your work.'

Travis didn't feel well. He stuck the gun in his belt. The barrel felt warm. He turned to Annabelle. 'You alright?'

'No,' she said, unsurprisingly.

Travis freed her from the ropes around her wrists and ankles, then he helped her to stand. She didn't appear to be any taller than he remembered so he presumed the rack hadn't been put into use. 'Any major injuries?' he asked her anxiously.

She shook her head. 'They merely beat me. They were waiting for the Prince to arrive before they got down to the serious business.'

'The Prince . . .' Travis glanced towards the door. 'He could turn up at any moment.'

'Nah,' said Jack, 'he's too busy supervising the search for us. And don't forget he's got a siege to contend with too.'

'He'll come,' said Annabelle quietly. She was rubbing her

arms, her face drawn and grey in pallor. 'No matter how busy he is, he wouldn't forego the overseeing of my slow death. Such things give him great pleasure.'

'She's right,' said Sharon. 'From what I know of Prince Val he'll show here sooner or later.'

Travis thought for a few moments. 'Okay then, let's prepare a welcome for him. First we'll have to hide those two . . .' He pointed towards the two dead torturers.

Jack fluttered across the dungeon. 'There's some kind of trap door over there,' he called.

Travis investigated. There was a circular wooden grating set in the floor with a metal ring on one side. Travis tugged on it. Slowly he managed to haul up the grating, then let it fall backwards with a crash. He peered into the darkness below but couldn't see anything. He looked at Annabelle. 'Do you know what's down there?'

She shook her head.

'Jack, would you mind flying down there and checking it out?' he asked.

Jack said, 'Travis, would you mind if I stick your testicles in a meat grinder.'

'I'll take that as a "no", then.' Travis continued to peer down the shaft. 'It might be a short cut out of the castle,' he mused.

'I think that's highly unlikely,' said Annabelle grimly.

He sighed. 'Yeah, you're probably right. Sharon, give me a hand with the two stiffs. We'll throw them down whatever this is.'

He and Sharon dragged the first of the two corpses over to the hole then shoved him into it. After a pause came the sound of a splash. Then came other sounds. The sounds of munching.

'Obviously the castle's garbage disposal unit,' said Jack.

Something in the depths burped loudly. Travis shuddered. 'Okay, let's do the other one.'

When they'd disposed of the second body in a similar fashion, Travis closed the grating with relief. 'Now let's hide and wait for Prince Val . . . Um, hang on, I've just thought of something.'

'You want to go back for the toilet rolls?' suggested Jack.

Ignoring him, Travis looked at Annabelle. 'I want to ask an enormous favour of you,' he told her.

'Hell, this is no time for a screw,' said Jack. Still ignoring Jack, Travis said to Annabelle, 'I want you to get back on the rack.'

Her grey pallor faded to white. 'What?' she gasped.

He took hold of her hands. 'Think about it. The first thing the Prince will see when he comes through the door is the rack. And when he doesn't see you on it he's going to know something's wrong and come to a dead halt. He'll call out for his two defunct minions and when he doesn't get a response from them he'll be even more suspicious and probably get the hell out. I need him to come all the way in. Understand?'

She simply stared at him.

'I promise you I won't let any harm come to you,' said Travis.

'Uh oh, that means you're dead meat, babe.'

'Shut up, Jack!'

'I'll do it,' said Annabelle, softly.

'You will?' said Travis, surprised. 'Good . . . good. Come on, let's hurry . . .'

As Travis loosely rebound Annabelle to the rack, Jack said, 'He's not likely to come alone, you know.'

'Yes. But he'll only have a couple of men, surely,' said Travis. 'And we can handle that, eh Sharon?'

The succubus gave him a smile that revealed her sharp teeth.

Travis finished tying up Annabelle. 'Comfortable?' he asked her.

'No,' she said.

'Oh . . . well, I guess you're not supposed to be. I mean, the whole point of a torture rack is . . . look, hopefully it won't be long.' Travis quit while he was ahead, gave Annabelle a reassuring pat on the shoulder and then turned to Jack. 'Jack, knock out a few of those torches will you? I want to make the place even gloomier than it is. Then we get into position . . . and wait.'

*

Travis estimated it was about half an hour later when the Prince entered. Travis was relieved to see that he was alone. The Prince came straight towards the rack and Travis ducked his head down.

'Sorry to keep you waiting, Annabelle,' he heard the Prince say, 'but I was unavoidably delayed.' There was a pause. 'Maurice? Jeremy?' the Prince called, 'Where are you?' When there was no response the Prince said, 'Annabelle, where is that pair of cretinous posing pouches?'

'I don't know,' she murmured.

'If they've sneaked off to the beer cellar again I'll have their skins . . .'

Travis stood up and pointed the Colt at the Prince. 'That's already been taken care of, Val. Maurice and Jeremy are not only *sans* their skins, they're *sans* everything.'

The Prince betrayed only a brief flicker of surprise before regaining his composure. 'Well, well, you again. You really are becoming a nuisance, Travis.'

'We aim to please,' said Travis as Jack flapped into view and Sharon also emerged from the shadows. The Prince glanced towards them. 'So this is where you have got to, Sharon,' he said. 'You'll be interested to hear that Damion is very anxious to recover you.'

'He's not dead?' she asked.

'No. He's got a very sore head but he's far from being dead.'

'Pity.'

'Jack,' said Travis, 'untie Annabelle, quickly.'

'Sure thing,' said Jack and landed on the rack.

'I don't see why you're going to all this trouble,' the Prince told Travis. 'You can't get away. Your position is hopeless.'

'Not completely. We have you.'

The Prince gave a small snort of contempt. 'Have you indeed? You think I am intimidated by your pathetic talisman?'

Released from her bonds again, Annabelle quickly got off the rack and stood beside Travis. She was trembling with fear. Travis said, 'I think you're very intimidated by it.'

'Nonsense,' said the Prince, smiling. 'You can't kill me. As you insist on telling all and sundry – I am a vampire.'

'But you're not immortal. Damion told me that.'

'True, but I can't be killed while I am under contract to the King of the Vampires. I estimate I'm good for another sixty years. After that I become a mere mortal again. Kill me then, if you can wait so long.'

Uh oh, thought Travis.

'He's bluffing,' said Jack. 'That Colt isn't of this world. It's immune to the magic here. You know that . . . and so does he.'

'The flying armpit spouts rubbish,' said the Prince in a bored tone.

'Let's test it out, shall we?' said Travis, gripping the Colt with both hands. 'Let's blow a few major holes in you and see what happens.'

The Prince took a step backwards, his composure suddenly slipping drastically. 'Er, let's not be too hasty . . . Having holes in me would be rather inconvenient . . . it would take hours to heal them . . . and besides, this is my favourite suit!'

'Ahah,' crowed Jack, 'I was right! Look, Val's practically pissing himself!'

Travis gestured with the gun. 'Not another step or I start firing!' he warned the Prince.

The Prince put his hands out. 'Please . . . don't . . .'

'And no vampire trickery either – like trying to turn yourself into a bat or something.'

The Prince regained a little of his composure and said, sniffily, 'I don't do rodents.'

'Well, whatever you *do* do, don't try doing it.'

'Why don't you just kill him?' asked Annbelle.

The Prince gave her a hurtful look, 'Annabelle . . . after all I've done for you . . .'

'We need him,' Travis told her, regretfully.

'So you have me *temporarily* in your power,' said the Prince, becoming bolder by the second. 'But you're still in a hopeless situation. Where can you go? How can you get out of the castle? And supposing you do manage that, you'd still be surrounded by a hostile army.'

'I'll cross that drawbridge when I come to it,' said Travis, 'But right now we're going to pay a visit on Beatrice. And should we encounter your minions on the way make it very clear to them, very quickly, what will happen to you if they try to obstruct us. Understand?'

'Yes, I understand,' said the Prince, reluctantly.

'Good. Then let's go.'

The Prince knocked on the door and called, 'Beatrice? It's me, Valerie. Wake up!'

While they waited for Beatrice to respond, Travis checked the passageway in both directions but the Prince's men were obeying his orders and staying well clear.

The door opened and Beatrice peered sleepily out. Her hair was a mess and she was wearing an unflattering, crumpled sleeping gown but to Travis she was still the most beautiful creature he'd ever seen. She looked at the Prince and said, 'I keep telling you, Valerie, not until after we're married.'

Phew, that's a relief, thought Travis.

'Er, that's not the reason for my visit, beloved. And we're not alone.'

Beatrice opened the door wider and blearily inspected them one by one. Then she frowned, clearly a little confused as to why a committee consisting of the Prince, Travis, Jack, a blood-stained servant girl and a spectacularly naked woman should decide to pay her a visit in the early hours of the morning. 'Is something wrong?' she asked.

Beautiful indeed, thought Travis, *but definitely not the brightest thing on two legs*.

'Nothing's wrong,' said Jack. 'We just happened to be in the area and decided, on the spur of the moment, to pay you a social call, you nitwit.

'Can we come in?' asked Travis.

'*All* of you?' she asked, surprised.

'Yes, all of us,' said Travis.

'Well, I don't know,' she said doubtfully. 'It *is* rather late . . .'

Give me strength, thought Travis. He dug the muzzle of the gun harder into the Prince's ribs. 'Valerie . . .'

'It really *is* important that we all come in,' the Prince told her hastily.

'Well, if you insist.' Beatrice opened the door wide and stood aside. They all trooped inside, apart from Jack, who flew. Beatrice closed the door. 'Please make yourself comfortable,' she said, adding, 'Valerie, I'm so happy to see that you and Travis are friends again.'

Jack, after landing on the headboard of the bed, chuckled. 'Yeah, they're real bosom buddies.'

Beatrice stared doubtfully at Sharon. 'Would you like to borrow one of my gowns?' she said, in the tone she normally used for asking commoners what they did for a living.

'No. Why?' replied Sharon as she reclined across the bed. Travis would have found her pose unbearably provocative if he hadn't been so preoccupied with other matters.

'Well, it's just that you're not wearing any clothes,' Beatrice told her, redundantly.

'I never wear clothes,' said Sharon, taking an apple from a bowl of fruit next to the bed. 'Don't like them.'

'She likes to be inconspicuous,' said Jack.

'Ignore her,' the Prince told Beatrice, 'she's just Damion's bit on the side. A dirty little succubus.'

'Oh, really?' remarked Beatrice, trying to be polite. 'And what exactly is a succubus?'

'I'm a demon. I feed on men's souls,' said Sharon, taking a large bite from the apple.

'How interesting,' said Beatrice.

'Here's something else you'll find interesting,' said Travis, placing the muzzle of the gun against the Prince's neck. 'Tell her, Valerie.'

The Prince cleared his throat and said, 'Beatrice, my dear, I have a small confession to make.'

Chapter Seventeen

'You really *are* a vampire?' Beatrice asked.

'I'm afraid so, my dear,' said the Prince.

Beatrice thought for a while and then gave a little shrug. 'Oh well,' she said, 'nobody's perfect.'

The Prince beamed. 'How understanding of you, my darling! Then you'll still marry me?'

'Of course,' she said.

Travis groaned. 'Look, you twit, it's a bit more serious than being involved with a man who goes out a lot at night.' He prodded the Prince with the gun. 'Tell her the whole story. All of it.'

'Must I?' sighed the Prince.

Travis jabbed again, harder. The Prince told Beatrice of the family pact with the King of the Vampires and her eventual fate after she had provided him with a son.

She looked shocked. 'I don't like the sound of *that*,' she said, with masterly understatement.

'And this is the monster you were going to marry,' said Travis

'I'm very disapointed in you, Valerie,' she told him sternly.

'There's more. Take a look at poor Annabelle here. And that's *before* your husband-to-be got a chance to go to work on her. He planned to torture her to death tonight, until we interrupted him. And all because Annabelle tried to warn you about him.'

Beatrice gave Valerie a look of profound disgust.

He shrugged apologetically. 'I suppose this means the wedding's off?'

'Most certainly,' said Beatrice.

'A pity,' sighed the Prince. 'I imagine I must now hand you back to that doltish knight of yours. I don't want the inconvenience of having to defend the castle if you're no longer going to marry me.'

'You will not! Rodney would take me back to Vallium and my father.'

'I have no choice now but to comply with his demands,' the Prince told her, spreading his hands wide and shrugging. 'Since you are no longer of any value to me.'

'I'm not going back to Vallium,' said Beatrice firmly, 'I'm going to stay with Travis. I'll keep on travelling with him and his demon until I find a place of my liking to stay.'

The Prince laughed. 'Travis isn't travelling anywhere. He may have the upper hand for now, but he and his motley band are trapped in here, as you may have noticed. And sooner or later they will meet slow and painful deaths in the chamber where I encountered them.' He didn't seem too unhappy about that eventuality.

Travis transferred the gun to his other hand, then took hold of the barrel. He hit the Prince twice on the head with the butt. The Prince fell. 'He was beginning to seriously piss me off,' said Travis.

'You're getting good at that,' observed Jack, producing his pack of Marlboro. 'But he has a point. Where do we go from here?'

'I'm working on that.' Travis went to the narrow window and peered out. Beyond the moat, and no doubt beyond arrow range as well, he could see the camp fires of Rodney's surrounding army. Then he turned to Sharon. She had finished the apple, including the core. 'How small can you shrink people?'

'Oh, to about an inch, I suppose. Why?'

'I've had an idea, and it involves Jack . . .'

'It does?' asked Jack suspiciously.

'Yes.' Travis knelt down beside the prone Prince and began going through his clothes. 'Ah, this will come in handy,' he said, holding up a money pouch and shaking it. It made clunking sounds – gold coin sounds. 'We'll need this to buy horses and supplies in the town.'

'How are we going to get to the town?' Beatrice asked.

'Jack is going to fly us there. Now you'd better change into some travelling clothes, and find something suitable for Annabelle as well.' Beatrice looked at Travis disbelievingly.

'*I'm* gonna fly you there?' cried Jack. 'How do you figure that?'

As Beatrice rummaged in a large wardrobe, Travis was now removing a long lace from one of the Prince's boots. He tossed it to Jack who deftly caught it. 'What's this for?'

'Make yourself a cute little harness out of it,' Travis told him.

'Again, why?'

'Because we're going to need something to hang on to when we're riding on your back. After Sharon has shrunk us, of course.'

'Oh,' said Jack. 'Well, yeah . . . that might work okay.'

'There is a drawback,' said Travis. 'You'll have to carry the gun as well, since that can't be shrunk.'

'Shit, yeah, I don't think I could fly as far as the town carrying the colt.'

'Then you'll have to take rest stops along the way,' said Travis.

'Travis, would you and Jack please step outside for a few moments,' said Beatrice. She was holding a bundle of clothing in front of her.

He stared at her. 'Pardon?'

'I've found these old riding clothes. Please step outside into the passage while Annabelle and I change,' she said.

'Beatrice,' he said, speaking slowly, 'lurking out there is a whole bunch of your ex-fiancé's men. They are not happy bunnies. They're just waiting for the chance to fill me with arrows. And Jack. And you want us to step out into the corridor while you *change*?'

'I'm not taking my clothes off in front of you two,' said Beatrice firmly.

'Don't be ridiculous! There's already one extremely naked woman in this room and do you see anyone paying any attention to her?'

'I am,' said Jack as he fiddled with the boot lace. 'And I've seen the glances you keep giving her, dickwit. I'm amazed you haven't tripped over your tongue yet.'

'Oh good grief,' groaned Travis. 'Look, Beatrice, I'll shut my eyes. Now hurry up and change!'

'Promise not to look?'

'I promise,' he muttered through gritted teeth.

'You too, Jack,' said Beatrice.

'Hey, you know you can trust me, your babeness.'

'*Promise*, Jack,' she demanded.

'Just do it, Jack,' Travis told him, angrily.

'Okay, I promise too,' sighed Jack.

As Travis waited with his eyes shut he pondered on the possibility that there was a universal law about all princesses, no matter how beautiful, being absolutely infuriating.

'You can look now,' said Beatrice, a minute or so later. He looked. She and Annabelle were now wearing fetching breeches, tunics and boots. He glanced at Sharon. 'Are you sure you wouldn't reconsider wearing something, Sharon? You're going to, er, attract attention when we hit town . . .'

'Oh, and you think the rest of us *aren't* gonna attract attention, dickwit?' sneered Jack. 'We're just gonna sort of blend in, huh? And by the way, your use of "hit town" may not turn out to be metaphorical.'

'Don't worry,' said Sharon, 'I won't attract attention. I have a little trick.'

'And don't I know it, babe,' said Jack.

'No. I mean this one.' And Sharon abruptly vanished.

Travis stared at the now empty bed. 'That's some little trick,' he agreed.

'You can't see one single bit of me, can you?' came Sharon's voice from the bed.

'Nope. Do you have any other hidden talents?' asked Travis. 'Apart from your shrinking abilities and that feeding on mortal men's souls stuff?'

Sharon reappeared on the bed. She got off it and stretched herself in a way that made Travis think of a cat, among other things. 'I'm quite a good cook,' she said.

'Shall we stop chatting and get moving?' said Jack, tossing

his cigarette butt out through the window. 'It's gonna be sunrise soon and I don't want to be an even bigger sitting duck than I have to be.'

Travis went over to him and inspected the make-shift harness that Jack had cobbled together from the boot lace. 'Are those knots good and tight?' he asked.

'You'll find out soon enough,' said Jack and sniggered.

'Very reassuring. Now fly down to the floor and we'll get on board – after Sharon has shrunk us.'

Jack pointed at Valerie. 'What about him? You're gonna leave him alive? Or living dead, to be more exact.'

'I can't shoot him in cold blood.'

'*He's* the one with the cold blood.

'If you let him live he'll come after us, no matter how far we travel,' said Annabelle, 'I know him too well. He'll want revenge.'

Travis sighed. 'I know you're right. But. . .'

'*I'll* kill him,' said Sharon brightly. 'Give me your weapon.'

'Sorry. It won't work for you. I'm the only one who can fire the gun. And *that's* the only thing that can kill him.'

'So kill him,' said Annabelle, adding a plaintive, 'please.'

Travis shook his head. 'Sorry, I know he's a vampire and a downright sadistic monster but I just can't.'

'*You're* gonna be sorry, dickwit' said Jack.

'It really might be a good idea, Travis,' said Beatrice.

He looked at her in amazement. 'Beatrice, this is the man you were still prepared to *marry* even when you knew he was a vampire! And now you're asking me to kill him? I know you're fickle but this is ridiculous!'

'That was before I knew what he had planned for me. I won't feel safe now as long as he's alive.'

Travis looked at the unconscious Prince. He felt tempted, but he just couldn't. He shook his head again. 'Sorry.'

'Well, couldn't you just *damage* him a little?' asked Beatrice.

'Damage him? What do you want me to do – shoot off his big toe?'

'That would be a good start,' said Jack.

'Look, if he catches up with us I promise you all I'll kill him then,' said Travis.

'On behalf of everyone else,' said Jack, 'I'd just like to say how completely unreassured we are by those words.'

'Sorry, but that's the situation. Now shall we get going? Sharon, do your stuff.'

'What size do you want to be?' she asked

'Oh, about three inches will do.'

'Fine. Let's all hold hands . . .'

As Jack flew down to the floor, Travis, Sharon, Beatrice and Annabelle joined hands. 'Close your eyes, folks,' advised Sharon. 'Next stop, the basement.'

Travis put the gun down on the floor beside Jack, took hold of Sharon's and Annabelle's hands and closed his eyes. When he opened them again he found Jack looming over him. It wasn't a pleasant experience.

Jack grinned malevolently down on the shrunken foursome. 'Change of plan,' said Jack, 'I've decided to eat you all. Yum yum.'

'Very funny,' said Travis, in a voice that sounded perfectly normal to his own ears but must have resembled Mickey Mouse to Jack. 'Now turn round so we can come aboard.'

Jack did as he was told. They all clambered onto him and hooked their arms and legs through the harness. Travis chose to position himself between Jack's shoulder blades so that he could see where they were going. Beatrice joined him. 'Ugh, he smells even worse up close,' she complained, wrinkling her nose.

'I heard that,' said Jack. 'You can always get off and walk, Your Royal Highness.'

'Maybe Prenderghast will bring a can of deodorant the next time he pays a visit to deliver toiletries,' said Travis wishfully. The smell *was* dreadful.

'What's a "can of deodorant"?' asked Sharon.

'I'll tell you another time.'

'And don't forget you were going to tell me about "toilet paper" as well.'

'How could I ever forget that? Now, is everybody all secured?'

They all said yes. 'Okay, Jack, you may now take off.'

'Gee, thanks boss,' said Jack. He picked up the Colt .45 with a grunt. 'This is heavier than I remembered.'

'Will you be able to manage it and carry us as well?' asked Travis.

'We'll soon find out.' Jack spread his wings and they rose, shakily, into the air. The demon flew up to the narrow window and out through it. Then proceeded to drop like a stone towards the moat far below.

Chapter Eighteen

'Stop fooling around!' yelled Travis into Jack's ear.

'I'm not fooling around!' Jack yelled back.

'Oh . . .' The air was whistling by them as Jack fell. 'Flap your wings harder!' Travis yelled.

'Thanks for your advice, dickwit! I hadn't thought of that!'

But they continued to drop at a sickening rate. The moat was hurtling up towards them. Travis knew they would be in deep shit if they landed in it. Literally.

Then, mere moments away from disaster, Jack managed to slow the descent. 'Ooofff' he grunted as he strained his wings. To Travis's heartfelt relief, they were no longer falling but flying.

'Thank the Green Queen!' cried Beatrice with relief.

'How about thanking me, too,' gasped Jack.

But Travis saw that they were still not out of trouble. As they skimmed over the surface of the moat Jack was not managing to gain much height. And he was also flying very erratically, in a shuddering zig-zag course.

'Fly higher,' Beatrice advised Jack, somewhat unhelpfully.

'Listen, sister,' grunted Jack, 'open your yap again and you can swim the rest of the way.'

The bank drew nearer. Beyond it were the camp fires and tents of the Vallium army. 'Look out!' cried Travis.

Standing in the shadows on the bank of the moat was a man pissing into the water. He also appeared to be standing on crutches. 'What?' said Jack, who clearly hadn't spotted the man. When he did it was too late. Swerving to avoid the figure he flew straight into one of the man's crutches. With a wail, the figure toppled to one side. Jack made a crash landing on the moat bank. To Travis's relief, the demon stopped himself from rolling over and crushing his passengers. Even so it was a very bumpy landing and Travis felt extremely shaken by the time Jack had come to a grinding halt.

'Ow, my knees . . .' groaned Jack.

'Never mind your knees, are your *wings* okay?' Travis asked callously.

'I feel sick,' moaned Beatrice.

'Annabelle, Sharon – you okay?'

'I've suffered worse things tonight,' said Annabelle.

'It was fun!' said Sharon.

There was a loud groan. The fallen man was trying to stand up, using his remaining crutch for support. He succeeded, and then began to look around for what had hit him. Then he saw Jack. 'You!' he gasped. 'The wizard's pet demon!'

From the glow from the distant fires Travis could see the man's face. It was Rodney. 'Oh no,' Travis groaned as the knight limped awkwardly towards them. Travis noticed that Rodney had bandages on both feet now. 'Quick, get moving!' cried Travis to Jack.

'I'm a mess,' complained Jack, but he did start to scuttle away from the advancing knight.

'Where's your dastardly master, demon?' roared Rodney, 'If *you're* here then *he* must be close!' He took a swing at Jack with his crutch, which was a mistake since he fell over again.

'Take off! Take off!' yelled Travis.

'No, I'd prefer to stay down here running around like a headless chicken, dickwit,' gasped Jack, flapping his wings madly. At that moment he became airborne again, sort of. Rodney got to his feet and resumed the chase.

'Where is he? Where's your master?' cried Rodney as he hobbled after them waving the crutch.

'I wish he'd stop calling you that,' Jack gasped to Travis as he struggled to gain height. They were only about ten feet off the ground.

'Can't we go any higher?' cried Beatrice.

'Here she goes again . . .' groaned Jack.

'The gun! Use it on him!' Travis told Jack.

'You know I can't fire the damn thing . . .'

'No! Drop it on him! Get above him and drop it on his head.'

'Worth a try,' agreed Jack. He made a tight curve and headed towards Rodney. Just then Rodney took another swing with the crutch and by sheer luck hit Jack on the head. The next thing Travis knew they were plummeting towards the ground again. When they hit this time the lace broke and the harness fell apart. Travis found himself momentarily airborne once more before he landed amongst some reeds. The impact stunned him for a few seconds but, aware that he was quite likely to be stepped on at any moment by an enraged Rodney, he leapt back on his feet instantly, if unsteadily.

He could plainly see the giant knight but nothing else, so he climbed up onto a nearby stone and peered through the top of the reeds. He realized he'd been thrown some distance from where Jack had crash-landed, and could see no sign of the three women. Rodney was prodding at Jack with the tip of the crutch and shouting, 'Come on, you little piece of foul slime, tell me where your master is!' but Jack wasn't moving and appeared to be unconscious.

Travis jumped as a hand touched his leg. He looked down and saw it was Sharon, who seemed unharmed. 'Where are the others?' he asked. She gave a shrug, and joined him on top of the stone.

'If you don't tell me where your villainous master is then I'm going to beat you to a piece of demonic pulp!' cried Rodney, preparing to use the crutch again as a club.

Then Travis heard a voice cry out: 'Rodney, you moron, shut up and help me!' It was Beatrice.

Though her voice must have been faint to Rodney's ears he clearly heard something because he froze and stared down at Jack. 'Huh?' he said.

'It's me, *Beatrice,* you dolt! I'm down here! Stuck under Jack's leg! and phew, is it *smelly*!'

'Beatrice?' said Rodney wonderingly as he bent down over Jack. 'Can that be you?' He gingerly lifted one of Jack's legs and Beatrice crawled out. 'At last!' she cried.

Rodney reacted with horror. 'Beatrice! Oh no, what *have* they done to you?'

'What's it look like, you idiot?'

Rodney put the back of his hand dramatically to his forehead. 'But this is terrible! What fiendish wizard did this to you? Was it Travis, or the other one, Damion?'

'It was Sharon, actually,' Beatrice told him, brushing off her clothes.

'Fear not, my beloved!' cried Rodney. 'Though my quest may take me years and through every land in the world, I will find the means of lifting this curse from you! I swear it!'

'Oh, give me a break, you moron. I haven't *been* cursed . . .'

But Rodney wasn't listening, he was too busy emoting. 'No matter what dangers and perils I may face on my quest I shall not rest until I have succeeded in restoring you to your true size!'

Travis said to Sharon, 'Quickly, use your power to restore *me* to my normal size!'

She shook her head. 'Sorry. Can't do.'

'Why ever not?' he demanded.

'I'm about magicked out. Used up a lot of power to shrink all four of us. I've got to take time to recharge before I can grow anyone back up again.'

'And how long will that be?'

'Oh, about half an hour.'

'Shit.'

Rodney was now kneeling in front of Beatrice. 'I pledge to you, my Princess, that I will succeed in my quest. You have nothing to fear.'

'Right now the only thing I have to fear is *you*, Rodney. I know how clumsy you can be!'

'I'll pick you up, my beloved,' Rodney told her.

'No! *No,* You idiot! You'll crush me!'

But despite her protests he began to reach down for her. She hurriedly backed away.

Sharon said, 'There *is* a way I can recharge myself more quickly – but it will involve your help.'

'Great. What can I do?' asked Travis.

'You can make love to me.'

'Sounds good so far, but how will that help you recharge your powers?'

'Well,' she admitted, 'while we're making love I'll have to feed on your soul . . .'

'No way!'

'I'll only take a little, I promise. After all, I owe you.'

He shook his head. 'I'm not having my soul eaten, thank you.'

'It'll only be a nibble.'

'No,' he said firmly.

Rodney now had Beatrice in his hand and was lifting her upwards. She was screaming frantically. Travis was reminded of a scene from *King Kong*. 'Of course, you realize this means we'll have to postpone our marriage,' Rodney told Beatrice, 'with you being so small, consummation would be a serious problem . . .'

Beatrice screamed even louder.

'There is another possibility,' said Sharon.

'Does it involve my soul being served as a starter?' asked Travis suspiciously.

'Oh no. It's just that I may have enough power to make us a little bigger than we are now.'

'How big?'

'About two feet high. Two and a half feet tops.'

Travis thought about it. It was better than nothing, and he would be able to use the gun, providing he could find it. 'Okay then, let's try it.'

They jumped down from the stone. Sharon held his hands and he closed his eyes. When he opened them again both he and Sharon were above the reeds. 'Thanks,' he told the succubus. 'Try and find Annabelle while I deal with Rodney.'

He started towards Rodney and Beatrice, scouring the ground for the Colt. Maybe Jack was lying on top of it . . .

'Beatrice, will you please stop screaming,' pleaded Rodney, but to no avail. He still hadn't spotted Travis. Jack, meanwhile, was starting to stir. Travis saw, to his relief, that he had been right – the butt of the Colt was now visible beneath the demon. All Travis had to do was get to it. The problem was that Rodney was in the way . . .

'Rodney, put down that Princess!' he commanded, as loudly as he could.

Rodney turned and looked at him. 'Who the . . .?' Then he recognized Travis. 'It's *you*! The wizard! But you're a dwarf now!'

'I prefer the term, "person of restricted height", if you don't mind. Now put Beatrice down at once or I'll turn you into something really awful. Like maybe a Pekinese dog or a literary critic.'

Looking confused, Rodney backed away. Behind him, a dazed Jack was standing up. Travis desperately signalled to him, hoping he would get the message.

'I don't know what wicked wizardry you have performed on my beloved Beatrice,' said Rodney, 'but I will never again let her go.' With his free hand he started to draw his sword. And at that precise moment Jack hit him on his bandaged right foot with the butt of the Colt. It made a satisfying *crunching* sound. Rodney's subsequent shriek of pain was equally satisfying. But as he leapt into the air he not only dropped his sword back into its scabbard, he sent Beatrice flying skywards.

She screamed as she described a perfect arc through the air. Travis ran forward, cupping his hands to catch her. He was a big cricket fan but had been hopeless at the sport when at school. He had never once caught the ball. He hoped Beatrice would forgive him if he maintained his average on this occasion . . .

To his relief, and surprise, she landed right in his hands. He immediately swung them down and around, breaking her fall. Then he held her up in front of his face. 'Princess, are you okay?'

Her screaming was pretty loud for someone only three inches tall so he presumed she was alright.

Rodney was screaming too, hopping about on one foot and holding onto the one that Jack had whacked. That wasn't good. Pretty soon he would attract attention from the camp, if he hadn't already. Travis carefully placed Beatrice on the ground and told her, 'Don't move. Wait right here.' Then he hurried over towards the hopping Rodney, picking up the Colt from Jack on the way.

'You okay?' he asked the demon.

'You keep asking people that same damn fool question,' growled Jack, rubbing his head.

Travis went up to Rodney and punched him in the groin. This produced the correct reaction: Rodney went 'Ooooffff!' and doubled over, providing the diminutive Travis the opportunity of hitting him on the head with the gun. Rodney collapsed and went very quiet. *Jack's right,* thought Travis, *I am getting good at this.* He wasn't sure how he felt about that. He listened for the sound of approaching sentries but couldn't hear anything. But that didn't mean they weren't on the way . . .

Jack came over to the unconscious Rodney and kicked him in the side. 'Bastard! He almost killed me.'

Then Travis did hear a sound. He turned quickly but it was only Sharon. She was holding something in front of her. 'I found Annabelle. She's unconscious.'

Travis stared into Sharon's cupped hands at the tiny Annabelle. He could just make out the rise and fall of her chest. 'Annabelle,' he said softly, 'can you hear me?' But there was no response. He led Sharon back to where he had left Beatrice. Beatrice, he noted with relief, had stopped screaming. He knelt down in front of her. 'Beatrice, Sharon is going to put Annabelle on the ground next to you. She's been hurt. See if you can help her.'

'Of course. But Travis, I'm frightened. What are we going to do?'

As Sharon carefully set Annabelle down beside Beatrice, Travis admitted, 'I don't know. But we can't stay here.' He looked at Sharon. 'You recharged your magic battery yet?'

'No,' she told him, 'it'll take even longer now.'

'We don't have the time,' he muttered, 'even if they didn't hear him there's sure to be someone coming soon to see what's keeping him.'

'I *told* you how I could regain my powers,' said Sharon, meaningfully.

'Sorry,' he said, 'you're not nibbling on my soul.' Then he brightened. 'But there *is* an alternative!'

Chapter Nineteen

'Hey, Rodney, wake up! You've got work to do!' Travis slapped the knight across the cheek again. Rodney's eyes flickered open and slowly focussed.

'Gwrphherryporf,' he said. He said that because he had a gag in his mouth. His hands were tied behind him.

'Good boy,' Travis told him. 'Now I want you to just lie back and think of England.' Travis stood and said to Sharon, 'He's all yours.'

Sharon was on Rodney like a flash, attacking the knight's cod-piece with unholy zeal.

'Pzwergurguff,' said Rodney, eyes bulging with alarm.

Travis turned his back on the scene.

'Aren't you going to watch?' asked Jack.

'Of course not.'

'You're crazy. A chance to see Sharon in action is not to be sneezed at.'

'Thank you, but no thank you.'

'Look at that,' Travis heard Sharon say, 'it's the size of a limp peanut. This is going to be a real challenge. I guess it's a good thing I'm not my normal size because . . .'

'Spare me the intimate details,' Travis told her. 'Just get it over with as quickly as possible. And don't eat all his soul either. Remember you promised just to eat a little bit.'

'Spoilsport,' said Sharon.

'Pwfffugurfinggah!' said Rodney.

Slurping sounds ensued.

Feeling guilty, Travis went over to see how Annabelle was doing. He knelt down in front of Beatrice and Annabelle. 'How is she?' he asked Beatrice.

'She's made some moaning noises, but she hasn't come round yet. There's a nasty bruise on her forehead,' Beatrice said. Then she asked, 'What's Sharon doing to Rodney?'

'She's recharging her spiritual batteries,' he told her as he looked around. Still no sign of any of Rodney's men. Then he looked towards the castle. No sign of any activity there either, but their luck couldn't continue to hold. And very soon it would be dawn . . .

'She certainly looks very happy,' said Beatrice, 'but Rodney doesn't.'

Travis stood up. 'He isn't. She's eating his soul.'

'Well, she won't find *that* very nourishing,' said Beatrice.

Involuntarily, he glanced towards Sharon and Rodney. Sharon did indeed appear to be enjoying herself. He quickly looked away.

'Will you be much longer?' he called out.

'Nearly there . . .' gasped Sharon. A short time later she let loose with a piercing shriek. Alarmed, he again looked at the pair. Sharon was arching backwards on top of Rodney. The scream went on and on, then abruptly stopped. 'Got it,' she said, and rose up from Rodney. The knight moaned.

Travis didn't blame him.

'Way to go, babe!' cheered Jack.

'You're fully recharged?' Travis asked her.

'To the brim,' replied the succubus, licking her lips. She slowly started to grow until she was her normal size again. 'See?'

'Then let's hurry . . . Jack, tie up Rodney's feet, and then I want you to make another harness . . .'

Jack shook his head emphatically. 'No way, José. I can't carry you lot and that damn gun. We might cover a hundred yards, but then I'd be down again. It just won't work.'

'It will if you're bigger.' He turned to Sharon. 'Can you make him twice the size he is now?'

'I don't see why not,' said Sharon.

'Then do it.'

'Fine by me,' said Jack as Sharon took hold of his hand. She gave a frown of concentration and suddenly Jack began to grow. Very soon he was nearly as tall as Travis. Then Sharon looked up. 'Uh oh,' she said, 'there's trouble coming . . .'

'What kind of trouble?' asked Travis worriedly.

'Bad trouble . . . from the castle . . . it's flying towards us . . . better get ready to use your weapon, Travis.'

Then he heard it too. The flapping of powerful wings. But he couldn't see anything.

The gun . . .

He'd left it lying near Beatrice and Annabelle. It was so heavy to carry around when he was this size . . .

He ran to it. Lifted it. The flapping was very loud now. He looked up and saw a hazy dark form hurtling down towards them. He got an impression of huge, bat-like wings, claws and a long, narrow head that ended in a curving beak. Red eyes glowed above the beak. He fired the Colt. The recoil almost knocked him off his little legs but he was rewarded by the sound of a terrible scream of pain. He watched through the smoke as the huge but indistinct creature tried to fly away. It got as far as the moat before plummeting downwards. There was a loud, gooey splash, then silence.

'I hope that was Valerie,' said Travis.

'No. It was Damion,' said Sharon happily. 'I think you might have killed him. I can't sense his presence anymore . . .'

'Good. But now we've really got to move. That shot is going to attract attention. Jack, hurry up with that harness!' He could hear shouts coming from the nearest camp. 'Sharon, come here and shrink yourself and me down to three inches again.' He put the gun back on the ground as Sharon hurried over. Very soon they were the same size as Beatrice and Annabelle. He could see figures approaching from the direction of the camp. A voice called out, 'Sir Rodney, where are you?'

'Pwerfurglop!' said the knight.

Jack flew over and landed beside the foursome. He appeared vast now. 'It's a rush job but it should hold,' he said, referring to his new harness. He bent down so that they could climb onto his back. Travis and Sharon had to assist Annabelle who, though conscious now, was still very dazed and had no idea what was going on. Travis peered over the top of Jack's shoulder. The sentries had discovered Rodney.

'Sir Rodney! What happened to you?' asked the first guard to reach him.

'Pwizpulpolhgh!' Rodney told him angrily, trying to point towards Jack with his bound feet.

'Grab the gun!' Travis ordered Jack. Jack did so, then launched himself into the air. Now they had the attention of Rodney's men.

'Look! Over there!' shouted one of them.

'A demon!' shouted another.

'Shoot it!' shouted a third man, who Travis mentally crossed off his Christmas card list.

A cross-bow bolt whizzed past Jack but now he was gaining momentum and height. The increase in size had worked – he was now flying with ease, despite the weight of the gun. Two more bolts passed by but didn't come close to hitting Jack. Then they were out of range . . .

By the time they were flying over the town the sun was rising. After the chill of the ride through the night sky Travis enjoyed the growing warmth on his skin.

'We made it . . .' gasped Jack. 'Good thing too, I couldn't have gone much further . . .'

Travis directed Jack to fly to the stable where they had left Whiplash. Jack flew in through one of the stable's windows and landed in the straw. Travis and the women clambered down off Jack and were restored to their normal size by Sharon. When she'd finished, the succubus sat down wearily in the straw and said, 'I'm pooped. No one ask me to do anything else for hours.'

Travis was happy to see that Whiplash and Rodney's steed were still in the stable. He'd been afraid that the stable owner might have sold them off when he and Beatrice had failed to return. Walking over to Whiplash, he slapped him on the rump. 'Hello, Whiplash, old friend. Pleased to see me?'

Whiplash turned his head, looked at Travis and gave the horse's equivalent of a profound groan.

'Okay, everyone, we've got to get organized. We need more horses.' He took out Prince Valerie's money bag and opened it. 'I'll rouse the stable owner out of bed and buy two more from him . . .' He glanced at Annabelle who, though still looking shaken, was clearly feeling much better now. 'Can you ride?' he asked her. She nodded. 'Good. Beatrice, I want you and Annabelle to go to the inn and buy provisions – all you can carry – and get some wine, too.' He counted out some gold coins into her hand. She stared down at them with bemusement. 'I've never shopped before,' she said.

'Trust me, you and shopping were made for each other, Princess. After that we have to figure out where we're going to go. By now there are probably two armies on our trail. Who knows, maybe Rodney and Valerie have become allies . . .'

'They'd make a lovely couple,' muttered Jack.

'I know a place where we could hide,' said Beatrice, 'a place where they would never dare to follow us.'

'You do?' asked Travis. 'What is this place?'

'Mytherious Wood.'

'Mysterious Wood?' he asked, thinking she'd suddenly developed a lisp.

'No, *Myth*erious Wood,' Beatrice told him. 'They wouldn't follow us in there – it's the realm of the Green Queen.'

'The Green Queen? Her name's not Anita Roddick by any chance is it?'

'No, her name's the Green Queen. She's my favourite local deity. I've been praying to her for years. She's wonderful.'

'I see,' said Travis, though he didn't really. 'So why won't Valerie and Rodney, not to mention their armies, follow us into the Green Queen's Wood?'

'She wouldn't allow it. It would be a violation of her realm.'

'And what if Rodney and Valerie just don't give a damn and follow us anyway?' he asked.

'Then Mytherious Wood would destroy them. It can be a very deadly place.'

'Hmmmm,' he said, pondering hard, 'and how come the Wood won't destroy *us*?'

'Because we'd be throwing ourselves on the Green Queen's mercy. Also, she'd recognize me as one of her worshippers.'

'She doles out membership cards, does she?'

Beatrice frowned at him. 'What?'

'How will she know you're one of her worshippers?'

'She'll just *know*, silly,' Beatrice said impatiently. 'She's a *goddess*, for goodness sakes!'

Travis thought some more. Then, 'How far is this place from here?'

'About a three day ride.'

'And you know the way?'

'Yes.'

He sighed. 'Well, then, we might as well give it a go. Let's hope your Green Queen is as powerful as you say she is.'

'Oh, she's powerful alright,' said Beatrice. 'You'll see.'

'Doesn't look very mysterious to me,' said Travis, feeling disappointed. 'Looks like a pretty ordinary wood . . .'

They were on the outskirts of Mytherious Wood – at least according to Beatrice.

'Don't let yourself be deceived,' said Beatrice sternly. 'This is no ordinary wood. It's *The* Wood.'

'That all depends on whether or not you got mixed up on the way and this is some place entirely different.'

'I did not!' she protested. 'This *is* Mytherious Wood!'

'Okay, okay, don't blow your top.' He turned in his saddle and scanned the hilly landscape behind them. No sign of the three riders who had been following them for the last two days. He dismounted and began to lead Whiplash into the wood. Or Wood. 'Come on,' he said to the others, 'even if it's not Mytherious Wood we can still shake off the bad guys in here . . .'

'Wait!' called Beatrice. 'You can't simply walk in there like that! We have to make an offer to the Green Queen.'

'Fine!' he called back over his shoulder. 'You call her up. And you can tell her for me that I promise to shop in Body Shop for the rest of my life.' He was getting tired of all this mystical twaddle. He continued on into the wood . . .

And found himself sitting opposite Heather at a restaurant table. Heather was saying. 'Whatever is the matter with you tonight, Travis? I'm sure you haven't heard a single word I've said.'

He looked around him. He recognized the place. He was in the Red Fort indian restaurant in Soho, London.

He was *back*.

Chapter Twenty

He couldn't believe it. He was back in his own world! But how . . . ? He hadn't found any stupid Key. Unless . . . unless the Mytherious Wood itself had been the Key. He looked around the restaurant again and then back at Heather, who was frowning at him. She was wearing a white blouse and a black suede jacket. He looked down at himself. He was wearing a suit and tie. His favourite suit – the dark blue one. He felt his face. The familiar stubble had vanished.

'Sorry,' he told her, 'I was miles away.'

'You've been a real pain in the bum ever since you arrived,' she said irritably. 'I suppose it has something to do with Prenderghast.'

Travis flinched. 'Prenderghast!? How did you know about Prenderghast?'

'*You* told me, you twit. You've been worked up about your interview with the great man for days, but you won't tell me how it went this afternoon.'

'This . . . afternoon?' His head spun. 'Er, look, Heather, this may sound like a stupid question, but what day is it?'

She gave him an uncomprehending look. 'It *is* a stupid question. It's Tuesday, of course.'

'No, no. I mean the date.'

'You want to know the date? Are you alright, Travis? You weren't hit by a car or anything today, were you?'

'No. And I haven't fallen off my damn horse either.'

'Your horse? You don't own a horse.'

'Not any more, thank God. Now just tell me the date, please. Humour me. I have a good reason.'

'If you insist. It's the twelfth of January. You want to know the year as well?'

'The twelfth of January?' he repeated, wonderingly. The *same* day that he visited Prenderghast! But *months* had passed on Samella . . . how could that be? Had Prenderghast sent him back through time? Or had it all been some kind of weird delusion? Maybe Prenderhast had hypnotized him? But it had all seemed so *real*! He couldn't believe he'd thought all that.

'You've gone quiet again,' accused Heather. 'And you've got that funny look back in your eyes.'

He snapped out of it. 'Sorry. But I had a very strange experience . . . today. And it involves Prenderghast . . . I think.'

'Tell me about it,' she said.

'I will, but first I have to go to the bathroom. Excuse me . . .' He rose and headed quickly for the men's toilets. Once inside he stared at himself in the mirror. Then he threw cold water on his face. He tried to make sense of it all . . . and failed. What if it *had* been real? What if Prenderghast really was some kind of sorcerer who had banished him to that distant world and then brought him back? That meant he'd deserted Beatrice, Annabelle and Sharon when they were in serious trouble. But then they'd reached the Mytherious Wood and according to Beatrice they'd be safe there from Rodney and Valerie, so he had no real reason to feel guilty. Even so he'd never see Beatrice again . . .

He sighed, then opened one of the cubicle doors. He stared in admiration at the toilet, then, almost lovingly, flushed it. He really was *home*.

He returned to the table and sat down.

'Well?' said Heather impatiently. 'Tell me.'

He was wondering how to go about it when a waiter appeared at the table. 'Are you ready to order, sir?'

He looked at the menu lying on the table in front of him. If he'd read it he couldn't remember. He told the waiter they needed a little more time. The waiter left.

'Well? I'm waiting. And I'm also getting very hungry, so make it quick,' said Heather.

Quick? Travis breathed deeply. 'Well, it all began in Prenderghast's office. I'd made my accusations and he'd got very angry . . .' Just then someone tapped him on the shoulder. He thought the waiter had returned. He turned to tell the man they still weren't ready to order . . . and saw it wasn't the waiter after all.

It was Beatrice.

'Come on, Travis,' Beatrice told him. 'You have to come back with me.'

'Beatrice!' he squeaked. '*You* can't be here!'

'Well, I am.'

Heather was staring at Beatrice with a stunned expression. 'Travis, who is this? And why is she dressed like the Principal Boy in *Dick Whittington*?'

Then Sharon appeared beside the table, spectacularly naked as usual. There were gasps around the restaurant.

'Sharon . . .' said Travis weakly.

'Beatrice is right, Travis, you've got to come with us.'

A waiter hurried over to her, his intention obviously being to drape his jacket around her. She floored him with a single punch. More shocked gasps.

'Travis, what *is* going on?!' demanded Heather.

'I wish I knew . . .' he groaned. He shut his eyes, hoping it would all go away.

It did.

'Travis, are you alright?'

He opened his eyes again. The restaurant, and Heather, were gone. He was in bright daylight . . . on the outskirts of Mytherious Wood. He was sitting on the ground. Beatrice and Sharon were standing over him. 'I was back home,' he wailed, 'and you two brought me back here! Why? Why couldn't you have left me where I belong?'

'You know you can't go back, dickwit,' said Jack, perched on Whiplash's head. 'You can't go back until you find the Key.'

'You didn't go anywhere,' said Beatrice. 'When Sharon and I caught up with you in the Wood you had gone into some kind of trance. We had to drag you back out of the Wood . . .'

'No. I really was back in the real world! I saw a flush toilet and everything! You saw the restaurant! You and Sharon were there!'

'When we grabbed you we briefly shared in your delusion, that's all,' said Beatrice. 'You were being punished by Mytherious Wood. You didn't show proper respect for the Green Queen. If we hadn't been here you would have been trapped in your own delusion until you starved to death.'

'Oh . . .' said Travis weakly. But it had all seemed so real . . . the toilet, Heather . . .

Annabelle, still mounted on her horse, said, 'We can't stay here for much longer. Look.' She was pointing to the hills behind them. A whole row of outriders was visible on the skyline. They were about twenty minutes ride away.

Beatrice immediately got down on her knees facing the Wood. 'Oh great Green Queen, please hear this plea from one of your most devoted believers – we beg you to grant my companions and myself sanctuary within your Mytherious Wood. If you do so, we promise to obey your slightest whim.'

We do? thought Travis worriedly.

Beatrice rose to her feet. 'Come on.'

Travis rose also. 'Is that it? Did you get an answer?'

'Not in so many words,' admitted Beatrice as she began to lead her horse in the Wood, 'but we'll soon find out if our plea has been turned down.'

Travis hesitated before following her. He wondered if he'd find himself back in the Red Fort restaurant again.

'I hope this Green Queen doesn't have a thing about demons,' said Jack.

'And succubi,' added Sharon.

'Oh, she's very tolerant of people's different beliefs, just as long as you show her respect,' said Beatrice.

'And obey her slightest whims,' muttered Travis.

The deeper they penetrated the Wood the more that Travis saw that his initial opinion of the place was wrong. There was definitely something very strange about it. The trunks of the trees twisted and curved in such a way as to suggest the bodies of women. There were strong, sweet and vaguely erotic aromas in the air and Travis kept seeing movement out of the corner of his eye but when he turned to look at it directly he couldn't make out a thing. He also thought he could hear girlish laughter. Sometimes it sounded far off, but at other times startlingly close by, causing him to jump, although once again nothing was visible.

'Wood nymphs,' explained Beatrice when he asked. 'Dryads and sprites. They serve the Green Queen.'

'Shy little buggers, aren't they,' said Travis.

'These babes naked?' asked Jack.

'Usually,' said Beatrice.

'HEY, GIRLS, COME AND MEET YOUR UNCLE JACK!'

'Hush!' warned Beatrice. 'Don't do that! If you offend the entities that inhabit the Wood it could be very dangerous for all of us.'

At that moment came the sound of something very large moving through the bracken and bramble ahead of them. And it was coming straight towards them.

'Ooops,' said Jack.

They halted and waited. The sounds grew louder. Travis took out the Colt and turned the safety catch off. 'If we survive this, I'm going to jump on your packet of Marlboro,' Travis whispered to Jack.

A shape could now be discerned approaching them through the trees. It was huge. And as it drew closer Travis could begin to make out details.

'Bloody hell,' he muttered.

It was in the shape of a man, but a man over ten feet tall. And it wasn't a man. Its body consisted of pieces of branches, bark, leaves and growing plants. Its huge hands and feet were tree roots and its vast head was concealed by a grotesque, leering wooden mask. It stopped a few yards in front of them and regarded them in ominous silence. Travis seriously doubted if the Colt could do the thing any damage at all. It would be like firing at a wood pile. Then he noticed that a bird had built its nest on one of the creature's shoulders.

Unexpectedly, Beatrice stepped forward and said in a loud, and only slightly trembling, voice, 'We apologise for intruding, and for any offence we might have caused. We are supplicants to the Green Queen. We seek her protection.'

The Thing from the Garden Centre, as Travis was beginning to think of it, remained silent. Nor, thankfully, did it resume its advance.

'We throw ourselves on your mercy,' Beatrice told it.

More silence.

'It looks like the monster we built for *Swamp Creature* back in '79,' whispered Jack, 'only done with a much better budget.'

'Shut up, Jack,' whispered back Travis.

'Er,' said Beatrice, to the thing, 'I don't suppose you could direct us to the Palace of the Green Queen? Please?'

For a time there was again no response, then the thing suddenly spoke. Its voice sounded like two logs being ground together.

'It'll cost you.'

'It will?' said Beatrice, sounding surprised. 'How much?'

'Ten gold pieces,' rumbled the thing.

'What?' exclaimed Jack. 'That's highway robbery!'

'Shut up, Jack!' said Travis.

'Pay him, Travis,' ordered Beatrice.

'Ten gold pieces for some lousy directions? It's outrageous!' cried Jack.

'*Shut up, Jack!*' said Travis, Beatrice, Annabelle and Sharon in unison. Travis produced Prince Valerie's purse and counted ten gold coins. He advanced nervously towards the creature. 'Here . . .'

The thing held out its huge, gnarled hand. Travis dropped the coins into it. The hand closed round the coins with a cracking sound.

'Thanks,' said the thing, and with its other arm pointed into the woods. 'Keep going the way you were until you reach the Great Standing Stone, then do a sharp left and walk for another half a mile. Then you'll see the Queen's Palace. You can't miss it.' Then the thing slowly turned and strode off through the bracken.

When it had vanished from sight Jack muttered, 'Ten gold pieces for *that*. What a con-man.'

'We're lucky he didn't rip us to pieces,' Travis told him angrily. 'If we meet any more denizens of the Wood just hold your bloody stupid tongue, or it'll get ripped out.'

But they reached the Great Standing Stone without any further encounters, though Travis continued to see moving shapes out of the corners of his eyes, and hear voices. The Standing Stone turned out to be a large black rock that stood some thirty feet tall. It reminded Travis of one of the stones of Stonehenge, but far bigger. As he approached it he became aware of a humming sound and sensed an electrical aura in the air.

'Don't go too near it,' warned Beatrice. 'It provides the basic energy to Mytherious Wood. If a mere mortal like you were to actually touch it you would die of pleasure.'

Travis stopped. 'Maybe some other time . . .'

They continued on, following the giant tree-man's directions. And as he promised, half a mile further on they saw it . . .

The Palace of the Green Queen.

Chapter Twenty-One

The Green Queen's Palace was a tree. Travis guessed that the base of the trunk must have been several hundred feet wide and he couldn't even imagine how high it was because the huge spread of branches and foliage blocked any view of its top. There was no way the could have failed to see it from outside the Wood and Travis presumed its concealment was an act of magic.

'It's wonderful,' whispered Beatrice in awe.

'It's sure one big mother of a tree,' observed Jack. 'I'd hate to have to sweep up the leaves in autumn.'

Travis said, 'Well, we're here. Now what?'

Suddenly they heard laughter from all directions. Travis and the others turned, and saw that they were surrounded – surrounded by a horde of mainly naked young women of varying sizes. A few wore dresses made of a silk-like diaphanous material. Some had wings. Most of them carried spears.

'I've died and gone to pussy heaven,' said Jack.

'Please Jack, no more comments,' Travis told him. 'Those spears look sharp.'

'The Wood nymphs . . .' said Beatrice. 'But where is their Mistress?'

'Right here, daughter.'

They turned back towards the Tree. Where there had been no one just moments ago there now stood the Green Queen.

She was a tall, imposing figure with beautiful yet haughty features. Travis could see why she was called the Green Queen: she was dressed in an emerald green gown, wore a cloak of green leaves, had luminous green eyes and green fingernails. Even her shoulder-length hair was green. And she carried a twisted wooden staff from which green leaves grew. *It could have been much worse*, thought Travis, *the*

Green Queen could have turned out to be a seasick Quentin Crisp!

Beatrice sank to her knees and bowed her head. 'My Mistress . . .'

The Green Queen came towards them. Travis saw that small plants sprung up from her footprints in the soil. He made a mental note not to shake hands with her. Then he flinched when she placed her hand on the back of Beatrice's head. 'Bless you, daughter. Now rise.' When she took her hand away Travis was relieved not to see an eruption of greenery through Beatrice's black hair.

As Beatrice stood, head still bowed, the Green Queen greeted them each in turn. 'Welcome Annabelle, Sharon . . . and hi Travis, how are they hanging?'

That caught him completely off-guard. 'I beg your pardon?'

She laughed. Her cloak of leaves rustled. 'I know where you're from. I've even visited Earth, but that was some time ago.' Then she gave a sigh, 'It's been a long time since I . . . met an Earthman.'

'Hey, I'm an Earthman too,' piped up Jack.

She looked down at him. 'You *were*.'

'So I had a bit of bad luck. Those are the breaks.'

She put her finger to her chin and looked thoughtful, then she suddenly touched him on the head with the tip of her staff. Jack disappeared.

In his place was a smallish, balding man in his mid-forties. He was wearing checked trousers, a maroon jacket and a black shirt. He was also wearing shades. He looked down at himself, patted his chest and said, in a deeper version of Jack's voice, 'Hey, I'm *me* again!'

'I'm afraid I can only remove the curse temporarily,' she told him. 'Once you leave my domain you'll become a demon again.'

'Who cares? This is great! Thanks a lot, Queenie!'

'It's Your Highness to you, Jack,' she said coldly.

'Sure. Sure. Anything you say. Sorry, Your Highness.' He took a packet of Marlboro out of his jacket pocket and nervously lit a cigarette with a gold lighter. The Queen gestured and the cigarette vanished.

'And this is a "No Smoking" zone,' she told him.

He grinned sheepishly. 'Fine with me, Your Highness. Sorry.'

'Now,' said the Green Queen, 'let us retire to my Palace. I'm sure you could all do with some refreshments.' She turned towards the Great Tree and pointed her staff at it. An opening appeared in the base of the trunk. *Like a human eye on its side,* thought Travis. *No, more like a vagina . . .*

The Green Queen said, 'Come,' and glided off towards the opening. Travis and the others followed her, taking care not to step on any of the small plants she left growing in her wake.

Inside the Great Tree, Travis saw that it appeared to be mainly hollow, or rather it contained a great space around which spiralled various structures connected by a series of gently sloping ramps. Wood nymphs were everywhere, some walking about, some flying – wings seemed to be an optional extra. Looking up at that vast space made Travis feel dizzy.

'Wow!' said Jack. 'This is even more impressive than the Los Angeles Hilton.'

'Before I offer you refreshments, I suspect you would like to know what your enemies are doing. Follow me.'

In the centre of the floor, which stretched away into the shadows, was a pool of water. 'Watch,' she instructed, and dipped her staff into the pool. There was a swirl of colour and suddenly they were seeing the view from the same section of the Wood that they'd entered. A large number of men and horses were now gathered on the slope of the hill. Like a movie camera the image in the pool 'zoomed' in on the row of men. It concentrated on two of them – Sir Rodney and Prince Valerie. As Travis had feared, their two enemies had united against them.

'Can you get sound on this gizmo . . . Your Highness?' asked Jack.

'Of course.'

'. . . And I still say we should simply ride straight in,' they heard Sir Rodney say. 'We have enough men.'

'No. You don't know the Green Queen as I do. She and this wood possess powerful magic. None of us would reach her Palace. I insist we wait for my sorcerer to arrive. We must fight magic with magic.'

'Rats,' said Sharon, 'that means Damion is still alive.'

'When do you expect him?' Rodney asked the Prince.

'Not until tomorrow. Travelling is not easy for him in his condition. In the meantime we might as well make camp.'

The Green Queen removed her staff from the pool and the image disappeared.

'Well, it sounds as if you wounded Damion seriously,' said Sharon to Travis, 'but he's still alive and that's bad.'

'I know little of this Damion,' said the Green Queen, 'except that he is very young.'

'Young but powerful,' said Sharon, 'and he's extremely devious.'

'Be easy,' the Green Queen told her. 'You're perfectly safe here.'

'I hope so,' said Sharon, not sounding convinced.

Travis shared her unease. 'Can't we launch a pre-emptive strike? Attack their camp in some way during the night and scatter them to the four winds . . . or something?'

The Green Queen shook her head. 'They must enter the Wood before I can act. But forget them for the time being. Now you must eat, drink and rest.'

'Now you're talking, Quee . . . Your Highness,' said Jack.

An hour later Travis was reclining on a couch made of soft green moss, a cup of potent cider in his hand. It was his third such cup. They had just finished an excellent meal – strictly vegetarian – served by a series of beautiful nymphs, and had then been invited by the Green Queen to relax in this soothing chamber which, the Queen announced, had been especially grown for them during the meal.

'This is the life,' said Jack, who was lying on a similar couch of moss. 'Thanks, babe,' he said to a nymph who was offering him a bunch of grapes. He took the grapes, winked at her and asked, 'You got any plans for tonight?'

The nymph giggled and left.

'Oh, man, look at the ass on that one,' sighed Jack, eyeing her retreating naked bottom. 'God, it's great being my old self again. I can't believe some of the disgusting things I got up to when I was a demon. I mean, I enjoyed eating *goats' testicle stew*, for Chrissakes!'

Travis still hadn't adjusted to seeing Jack as a human being, if you could call a sleazy producer of exploitation movies a human being.

'Jack, you're just as disgusting as a man as you were when you were a demon,' Beatrice told him.

'I know you don't really mean that, Princess,' said Jack, sounding hurt.

'I preferred you as a demon,' sniffed Sharon.

Another nymph appeared. She made straight for Travis. 'Sir, the Green Queen requests your presence. Please accompany me.'

'Me?' said Travis, surprised. 'She wants to see me?'

'Yes. In her private chambers.'

'Ooooh, boy, you could be onto a good thing here,' laughed Jack.

'Shut up, Jack,' said Travis as he rose from the couch. He wondered, a little nervously, what the Green Queen wanted with him.

The Green Queen's private chambers turned out to be like some kind of fairy grotto – which he supposed it actually was. There were plants and flowers everywhere and the light was soft and dreamy. There was perfume in the air, presumably from the flowers, and a sweet tinkling sound that reminded him of wind chimes. There was also – he had to admit it – *magic* in the air.

He followed the nymph through a series of translucent silken drapes of varying colours until they finally reached the Green Queen's inner sanctum.

It was like being inside a womb – not that Travis could

remember the last time he'd been in one, but he had a definite feeling it must have been like this. The organic chamber, with its sloping walls and tangle of twisting roots and luxuriant vegetation seemed to pulsate with a comforting and reassuring heartbeat. Dominating the chamber was a large circular bed consisting of a cluster of branches that spread from a single thick wooden trunk that grew from the floor. The array of branches supported a round white pad of some sort of soft material. Lying on this was the Green Queen.

She had changed her attire. She no longer wore the robe and the cloak of leaves – instead she was covered from neck to feet with thousands of small green leaves that appeared to be glued to her body. And Travis could now see it was *some* body.

'Welcome, Travis,' she said. 'Please sit down. No need to be formal with me here.' She indicated, with a languid gesture, a chair that he hadn't noticed before. As he sat down it seemed to mould itself to his body, becoming incredibly comfortable. 'Tyra,' she said to the nymph, 'please fetch us some wine.'

'Yes, Your Highness,' said the nymph and vanished.

The Green Queen sat up on the bed and crossed her legs. It seemed to Travis a very un-goddess thing to do.

She said, 'You have questions for me, and I have questions for you.'

'You do?' he said, surprised. 'I was under the impression you knew everything.'

'Hardly,' she said, and laughed. 'What I know about you I learned from the mind of my worshipper, Beatrice. But there is much I don't know about you, apart from the fact that you and your companion, Jack, have had an encounter with One of Us, otherwise you wouldn't be here.'

'One of Us?'

She nodded. 'A being like myself. A supernatural entity. Someone who can span the Variations of Existence.'

'Yes . . . he calls himself Prenderghast. But he's nothing at all like you, Your Highness.'

She laughed again. 'Oh, call me Megan. That's the name I used when I visited Earth. And yes, I've heard of Prenderghast. Very old, very powerful and very mean. How did you come to earn his displeasure?'

Travis told her the story. While he was relating it the nymph returned with two goblets of red wine. It was delicious, of course.

'And Prenderghast gave you no indication of the nature of this Key you must find?' she asked when he had finished.

'None at all. But perhaps it doesn't matter anymore. Surely *you* have the power to send me back to my world?'

'No,' she said, dashing his hopes. 'I can no more undo what he has done than he could overturn my power. As I told Jack, I can only temporarily lift the curse placed on him. And I can do that because he is in my domain.'

'I see,' he said, regretfully.

'I'm sorry. Now, do you have any other questions?'

'Yes. Tell me, is this all *really* happening? Or . . . ?'

'Or is it all some induced dream you're experiencing against your will?' she said and smiled. 'How can you believe any answer I can give to you? I'm part of the experience. I'm hardly going to tell you I don't really exist.'

'I don't care . . . just tell me – *is* this place real?' he asked, pleadingly.

'It's as real as your world, and how real is that?'

'Good question,' he said with a sigh. 'Okay, another question: why does he do the things he does?'

'Prenderghast?'

'Yes. What's he up to?'

'He's feeding.'

'Pardon?'

'He needs to feed in order to survive and maintain his power.'

'Feed on what?'

'People. Oh, I don't mean he actually *eats* people physically, but he feeds on their life forces. I derive my power from the love of my worshippers but Prenderghast has chosen to go along his own path, therefore he steals the power he needs. Tricking unwary people into letting him feed upon them.'

Travis felt shocked. He remembered Prenderghast's virtual reality helmets, for children. He sat up in the chair. 'I've got to get back there! I've got to stop him! Expose him to the authorities . . .'

'Travis, you know you can't return until you find the Key.'

He slumped back. 'Yes . . .'

'I've been thinking,' she said slowly, 'and I may be able to help you there.'

'You'll help me find the Key?'

'Yes, I think I know where it might be located.'

'Where? Where?' he asked, eagerly.

'Ah, but first you must perform a service for me.'

'Oh, yes?' he said, instantly suspicious. 'Like what?'

'I want you to make love to me.'

He thought that over. There had to be a catch. 'So you can feed on my soul or my life force? No way.'

'I assure you it's nothing like that. I only want one thing from you.' She stood up on the bed. The tiny leaves began to fall from her body. More and more fell away, until they formed a green cover across the bed and she was completely naked. 'I want your seed.'

He noticed that her nipples and pubic hair was also green but, heck, this was no time to be fussy.

Chapter Twenty-Two

'Damion's there somewhere,' said Sharon, 'I can *smell* him.'

It was the following day and they were gathered again on the edge of the Green Queen's magic pool of water. The image in the pool was of the massed ranks of Sir Rodney's and Prince Valerie's armies. There were three times as many men as there had been the previous day. Travis didn't feel in the slightest way apprehensive. He was quite light-headed, his blood still singing from his night with Megan, or rather the Green Queen as she was once again. Having sex with a goddess was definitely the experience of a lifetime but he wasn't sure he would want to make a habit of it. For one thing he didn't think his heart would last the distance. He wondered what use she planned to make of his 'seed' but as she hadn't volunteered the information he hadn't had the temerity to ask her outright. Would he one day, unknowingly, be the father of a grove of fine young saplings?

'Something's happening, folks,' announced Jack.

Travis peered into the pool. A small group of men had emerged from the long row of soldiers and was moving down the hill. Two of the men were carrying another man sitting in a chair. 'Can we close in on them, Your Highness?' asked Travis.

The Green Queen obliged. They had a close-up of the group. 'It's Damion!' cried Sharon.

'And boy, does he look crummy,' said Jack.

The man being carried in the chair *was* Damion, but he appeared to be a shadow of his former self. He was gaunt and pale and looked much older; his left arm hung in a black leather sling and his right eye was covered by a black patch. A blanket covered his legs.

'You sure messed him up, Travis,' said Sharon. 'But unfortunately the son-of-a-bitch is still alive. And dangerous.'

I'm curious to know what he plans to do,' said the Green Queen, unconcernedly.

The soldiers carried Damion to the base of the hill and then carefully settled his chair on the ground. Damion's single eye glared balefully, and he spoke. 'I know you're watching me, Green Queen!' he cried, his voice cracking from the strain, 'And perhaps the loathsome enemies that you recklessly shelter are watching this too! Good! I want you all to witness the beginning of your complete and utter destruction!'

'He's definitely lost his sense of humour,' said Sharon.

Damion reached under the blanket across his lap and produced a small, black leather bag. He gestured to the soldiers and one by one they stood before him as he emptied something from the bag into their hands. They spread out in all directions and began scattering whatever it was that Damion had given them over the ground as if sowing seeds, which, it turned out, they were. Damion then beckoned them to stand well back. 'I scoured all the Variations of Existence for creatures that possess the most aggressive and repulsive characteristics – creatures that will prove unstoppable. I found two such species and combined them into what you are about to see . . . watch!'

Something broke through the surface of the ground and started to grow. Then another one appeared, and another . . . very soon there were hundreds of the things growing out of the earth in front of Damion. After another minute or two they were fully formed. They appeared to be part-trolls, with knobbly grey skins and horns, but these weren't the characteristics that chilled Travis to the bone . . .

It was the fact that they wore scarves, and large boots, had mean, blank eyes, low foreheads covered in Union Jack tattoos, and that their knuckles nearly touched the ground. It wasn't so much the portable rocket launchers and flame throwers that worried Travis profoundly, but the fact that many of them were clutching lager cans. And when they began their terrible chant, Travis's worst fears were confirmed.

The chant went: ' 'Ere we go! 'Ere we go! 'Ere we go!' And so on. Endlessly.

'They're based on English football fans,' Travis told the Queen. 'We're doomed.'

'Will they be a problem?'

'A problem?' Travis cried. 'Back on Earth they've laid waste to half of Europe!'

'No matter who they are, they won't be able to resist the magic of my Wood,' said the Green Queen.

'I wouldn't bet on it, Your Highness. For Mytherious Wood to weave a spell on somebody you need that person to have a mind. These creatures don't have minds! Their brains are second-best to an amoeba's!' He looked back into the pool. The troll/football supporters were starting to advance towards the Wood.

'I'll have my nymphs attack them with their spears,' said the Green Queen.

'Oh no! If that lot get a sight of your nymphs then all hell will be let loose. Believe me, you don't know what you're dealing with!'

'What do you suggest?'

'That jolly green giant who gave us directions – do you have control over him?'

'Of course.'

'Then get him moving to head them off. It will only be a delaying tactic, I'm afraid, but anything that gives us a bit of extra time is worth trying.'

The Green Queen put a hand to her forehead and closed her eyes. 'He hears and will obey,' she said.

Travis knew the feeling. He looked into the pool again. The first of the chanting mob of troll/football fans had almost reached the edge of the wood. Behind them the human army began to descend from the hill. 'See. Damion's plan is to use these monsters as an advance guard. They'll ravage a path through your Wood and the army of Rodney and Prince Valerie will be safe to follow.'

'We must stop them!' cried the Green Queen. She finally sounded alarmed.

'Have you got any more creatures like the Green Giant?' he asked her quickly. 'A man-eating cyclops, perhaps? The odd gorgon? A few minotaurs? A gryphon would be nice . . .'

She shook her head. 'No. I did have a minotaur once but it developed foot-and-mouth and I had to have it put down.'

Travis saw that the mob was beginning to enter the Wood. There were explosions as they began to unleash their rockets into the surrounding greenery. 'My poor Wood,' moaned the Green Queen.

Travis swallowed and drew his Colt. It looked rather small and ineffective compared to the firepower packed by the advancing army of football morons. 'I guess I can stop a few of them with this before they overwhelm me,' he said uncertainly.

'Don't be silly, Travis,' said Beatrice. 'The Queen will think of something. Won't you, Your Highness?'

The Green Queen was still staring at the grim images in the pool. 'Perhaps,' she began doubtfully, 'when they near the Great Standing Stone I can draw off a great burst of its energy to smite them down. But that would leave both me and the Wood very weak.'

'And you can't guarantee it would have much effect on them,' said Travis. 'No, it's up to me to try and stop them. It's my fault they're here, after all.' This sounded much braver than Travis felt.

'How do you figure that?' asked Jack.

'Damion wouldn't have known about Earth if I hadn't told him. He was hungry to get his hands on Earth weaponry, and now he has . . .' Travis paused, and then asked the Green Queen, 'He's not One of You, is he? Like you and Prenderghast?'

'Oh no,' she replied quickly, 'he's not One of Us. He's just an extremely powerful little shit.'

'Then maybe I can sneak by the invaders, get to Damion and blow him away. . .'

'You should have killed him when you had the chance,' Sharon told him.

'And Prince Valerie,' said Annabelle.

'Okay, okay, so I made a few misjudgements. You don't have to rub it in.'

'It wouldn't do any good now,' said the Green Queen. 'Killing Damion won't stop the terrible forces that he has unleashed.'

'Scrap that one then. Nothing for it but a direct attack.' Travis took a deep breath. 'Guess I'd better be moving then.'

'I'd come with you, buddy,' said Jack, 'but, you know, lookin' like this and without a weapon I'd just be a liability to you.'

'So what would be new?' asked Travis.

Before Jack could make a retort, Sharon said, 'I'll come with you, Travis.'

'Thanks for the offer, Sharon, but you don't have a weapon either.'

'I *am* a weapon.'

'Sharon, you eat souls. These *things* don't have souls.'

'I can help you in other ways,' she said, and promptly disappeared. 'I'd be your secret weapon. And admit it, you do need an ally,' came her voice from apparently air.

That was true, he thought. 'Yes, you're right. But the moment things turn seriously sticky, you get back here.'

'Sure,' she promised, popping back into view.

'Let's go then . . .'

'Good luck, Travis,' said Beatrice, 'I'll always remember you.'

'Me too,' added Annabelle.

'Hey, girls, do you mind not starting the wake until *after* I've died?'

'You have my blessing, Travis,' said the Green Queen, 'True, it's not worth a gnat's fart in this particular situation but the thought is there.'

'Thanks Meg . . . I mean, Your Highness.' He turned to go when he suddenly had an idea. 'I've just had an idea . . .'

'I hope that's one of those wild and crazy ideas where you add "and it just might work!" ' said Jack.

'I wouldn't go that far,' said Travis, 'but it's sure worth a try.' And he told them his idea.

'I like it,' said Jack. 'It's wild and crazy, but it just might work!'

'I'll get my girls started immediately,' said the Green Queen.

'I just don't understand it at all,' said Beatrice.

'I'll explain it to you later,' Travis told her, 'if there is a "later". Come on Sharon . . .'

Travis and Sharon hurried through the Wood towards the advancing horde of football trolls. They had no trouble locating the invaders' position – it was marked by a pall of black smoke. They kept being passed by frightened Wood nymphs, fleeing towards the doubtful sanctuary of the Green Queen's Palace. And in the background was the constant, dreadful chant: ' 'Ere we go! 'Ere we go! 'Ere we go!'

'We're getting close. Better do your disappearing act,' he told Sharon.

'Okay,' she said, but instead of abruptly vanishing as she'd done before, she faded away very slowly until only her nipples remained. Then they too faded out of sight. In other circumstances Travis would have given her a round of applause.

Travis, the gun in his hand, continued on cautiously through the trees. He could see the top of the Great Standing Stone ahead of him. 'By the sound of it, they've reached the Stone,' he told the invisible Sharon. 'Follow me . . .'

He pushed his way through a thick clump of bracken. From behind him he heard: 'Ouch! Ouch! Ouch!'

'Shush!'

'Do we have to come this way?' asked Sharon, plaintively.

'*I* do, not being invisible . . . but on second thoughts, you don't. So make your own way and catch up with me later.'

'Sure thing,' she replied, and Travis heard the bracken rustling as she retraced her steps, plus a series of little *Ouches*. He continued on towards the source of the nerve-grating chanting.

Finally he reached the clearing around the Great Standing Stone and peered cautiously out through the bracken.

A horde of football fans/trolls were dancing around a bonfire. A large, smouldering mask was sitting on the top of the burning pile of wood. Travis recognized the mask. The Jolly Green

Giant had clearly met his match, metaphorically and literally. Slogans were being crudely daubed on the sides of the Great Standing Stone in red paint from spray cans. Things like 'UP YORES!', 'BOLLOCKS!' and 'FOOK ALL FAIRIES!'

Behind the cavorting morons Travis could see the terrible swathe that they had cut through the Wood – a burned and trampled wound that stretched all the way to the edge of the trees. Mytherious Wood had been well and truly raped. And soon, along this swathe, the armies of Sir Rodney and Prince Valerie would begin their own penetration of the sacred Wood.

Anger filled Travis. Okay, so he was out-numbered three hundred to one – well, two if you counted Sharon – but he was determined to take out as many as he could before they overwhelmed him. And it would give the Green Queen some extra time to put his plan into action.

He hoped.

He took careful aim at one of the dancing football hooligan trolls and was just about to fire when he heard loud rustling nearby. A football fan/troll crashed out of the bracken only a few yards from where Travis was hiding. A terrified Wood nymph struggled in its huge arms. 'Hey, ya bunch of poofdahs! Look what I've got!'

The horde stopped dancing when they saw the Wood nymph and began cat-calling and yelling obscenities. Travis realized they would tear the poor nymph to pieces – if she was lucky. He stepped out of the bracken. 'Let her go, or you'll never read the *Sun* again!' Travis yelled.

The football fan/troll stopped and turned. 'Who the fookin' hell are you?'

'I said, unhand that nymph, or I'll kill you!' Travis could see that other creatures had also come to a stop, but he knew it would only be temporary. He had to act fast. The football fan/troll was large and the struggling nymph's head only came half way up his chest. There was no chance of hitting her so Travis fired, aiming at the creature's forehead. It was a perfect shot. A hole appeared dead centre.

Unfortunately the football hooligan/troll just continued to stand there! And he now looked very annoyed.

Chapter Twenty-Three

Shit! I must have missed his brain! Travis thought grimly, as the football fan/troll stayed defiantly on his feet despite the large hole in his forehead. *I knew their brains were small but not THAT small!*

'Ya fooker!' yelled the creature. Then it dropped the nymph, clutched at its head with both hands and said, 'Ow . . .' before toppling backwards. The freed nymph quickly scampered past Travis and disappeared into the Wood.

'The bastard's gone and killed Brian!' yelled a member of the mob. 'Get 'im!'

'Yeah! Kick his 'ead in!'

'Jump on his bollocks!'

The mob surged forward.

Travis stood and fired blindly into the advancing mass of baying, grey-skinned monsters. Then a hand grabbed the back of his collar. 'Come on, Travis!' he heard Sharon cry, 'Time to retreat!'

This advice struck Travis as incredibly sensible. He turned and followed Sharon – well, he presumed he was, as she maintained her invisibility – into the Wood. There was a whooshing sound and he saw a rocket whizz by him and hit a tree ahead. It'd passed so close to his head his right ear had been singed by its exhaust. The missile exploded, blowing the tree apart with a loud boom. The tree screamed as it died.

An invisible hand tugged on his sleeve. 'Into the bracken, quickly!' advised Sharon. Again, this struck him as very sound advice. He plunged into the bracken. Sharon was clearly doing the same because he could hear once again a series of soft *Ouches* coming from close by. He winced at the thought of what it must be like going through the thorny foliage stark naked. Maybe the experience would alter Sharon's attitude towards clothes.

' 'Ere we go! 'Ere we go! 'Ere we go!' chanted the pursuing mob. There were more explosions as they blew their way through the Wood.

Come on, Green Queen, do your stuff! prayed Travis. Suddenly he was all out of bracken. Ahead there was nothing but empty space between the trees for as far as he could see. 'Oh, rats!' he cried. 'We've lost our cover.'

'Frankly, I'm rather relieved,' said Sharon.

'It's okay for you. You're invisible,' muttered Travis darkly. He broke into a sprint. Then something happened to him that he'd only seen in old movies when women were running away from HIM, THEM or IT: he tripped over a dead branch lying on the ground and fell.

'Oooff!' he gasped as he hit the ground. The impact was softened by the layer of leaves that covered the floor of the Wood, but even so the gun went flying and landed a couple of yards out of his reach.

'There 'e is! Geddim!'

Glancing back, Travis saw two of the creatures emerge from the bracken. He scrambled towards the gun. *I need to tie the damn thing to my wrist!* he told himself angrily. Picking it up, he turned and looked again. The two football fans/trolls were lumbering towards him. He fired without taking careful aim and hit one of them in the arm. It didn't faze the creature for even a moment. Travis took aim before firing his second shot. The one he'd hit in the arm dropped to his knees, this time with a bullet between his eyes. But now the other one had almost reached him . . .

Suddenly, the very branch he'd tripped over flew up and smashed the creature across the face. He staggered back, his nose flattened. The branch hit him again. Sharon materialized holding the branch. The football fan/troll, despite the drastic deconstruction of what had passed for his face, managed to give her a lascivious look. 'Corr, you're a piece of orright, darlin',' he slurred. 'Fancy a quickie at 'alf time?'

Sharon hit him again and he promptly collapsed. Sharon grinned at Travis. 'This is fun!'

'I'm glad you're enjoying yourself,' said Travis, as he got up. 'You only have to do that again a few hundred times and all our problems are over . . .'

Travis heard the roar of a flame-thrower. A large section of bracken disappeared in a blaze of fire. And then the vanguard of the mob began to emerge from the charred and smoking vegetation. 'They're all your's,' Travis told Sharon as he backed away. Sharon dropped the branch and promptly vanished. Travis sincerely wished he could do the same.

' 'Ere we go! 'Ere we go! 'Ere we go!' chanted the advancing mob. Travis got ready to start running.

And then it began.

They began to fall from the sky. Cans. Gold cans. Lots of them. Soon they littered the ground between Travis and the horde of the football hooligans/trolls. The mob halted. Inevitably, one of the creatures picked up a can, pulled the tab on its top and took a tentative mouthful of its contents. There was a long pause as the others looked on expectantly. Then the football fan/troll announced his judgement. 'Fan – fookin' – tastic, lads!' he yelled, then drank down the rest of the can's contents in one long gulp.

With a loud roar, the rest of the mob pounced on the cans and followed his example. And when one can had been drained another one was quickly snatched up from the ground. More of the gold cans fell from the sky . . .

Travis leaned against a tree and surveyed the scene with satisfaction. The entire mob of football fans/trolls were lying sprawled out on the ground between the trees. From those few still capable of sitting up, there was a faint refrain of ' 'Ere we go . . .', but it was fast dying away. The amber liquid had done its work. Mentally challenged to begin with, the horde were now totally brain dead to a man, or troll.

Sharon, standing beside him and visible again said, 'Well, I've got to hand it to you, Travis, your plan did the trick.' She gave him a soft kiss on the cheek. 'Congratulations.'

'Thanks, but it was the Green Queen who made it work. Without her magic to speed up the brewing cycle and increase the beer's potency, we would have been finished.'

'Yes, but you were the one who knew those creatures' weak spot.'

'She's right. We are indebted to you.'

Travis gave a start. The Green Queen had suddenly materialized beside him. 'Your Highness . . .'

'Just one of my many talents,' she told him airily as she inspected the army of extremely pissed invaders. 'They are harmless now?'

'Yes. So it's time for Part B of the plan – send in the nymphs.'

Even though he suspected the football fans/trolls were the products of sorcery rather than actual living creatures he had to look away as the spear-wielding Wood nymphs began to finish off the invaders. Sharon, on the other hand, borrowed a spear and joined in the slaughter with gusto. 'What happens next?' he asked the Green Queen.

'With the destruction of these demon barbarians my Wood will mend its wounds – and recover its full power. Even now the human invaders begin to feel my wrath. Come, let us go and witness what has been wrought upon them. I'm sorry, but queens have to talk like that sometimes.'

The Green Queen took Travis by the hand and he found himself rising into the air beside her. Then they began to move forward, some ten feet above the ground. Travis felt like Margot Kidder in *Superman*.

Leaving the killing field quickly behind them, they followed the charred trail left by the invaders. Travis saw that already the Wood was repairing and reclaiming the demons' territory: green shoots were sprouting out of the blackness, and creepers were extending inwards from the Wood on both sides. When they reached the Great Standing Stone it was again humming with awesome power and Travis observed that the crude slogans and other daubed obscenities had vanished from its sides.

The Green Queen and Travis touched down beside the

still smouldering pile of burnt timber that had been the Jolly Green Giant. 'Poor Harry,' sighed the Green Queen.

'Who's Harry?' asked Travis.

'Him,' she said, pointing her staff at the scorched heap. Then she stepped closer and touched the heap with the tip of her staff. Almost immediately the mound began to stir. There were cracking and creaking sounds, and then greenery appeared. The charred outer casings fell away from the pile of logs and branches, revealing fresh green wood beneath. Slowly the mass assembled itself into the Jolly Green Giant. He adjusted his mask and then bowed stiffly, accompanied by a lot of creaking, to the Green Queen. 'Thank you, Your Highness. Sorry I let you down. The little bastards overwhelmed me.'

'No need to apologize, Harry. You did your duty.' She turned to Travis, 'Now let us fly on . . .'

The further they flew along the trail of devastation left by the football fans/trolls, the narrower it became. And eventually it disappeared altogether, the Wood having recaptured its lost ground. They touched down again and continued on foot. Travis could now hear the chilling sound of grown men sobbing and wailing. He glanced enquiringly at the Green Queen. 'The Wood has claimed them. The battle is over,' she told him.

Shortly afterwards they encountered their first soldier. He had lost his helmet and weapons and was blundering aimlessly through the undergrowth, arms held out in front of him. Tears were streaming down his face. He staggered past them, unaware of their presence.

'He is under the spell of the Wood,' said the Green Queen. 'And will eventually be absorbed by the Wood.'

'Rather him than me,' said Travis.

'There are *worse* fates,' she said, a tad imperiously.

They encountered more and more soldiers in a similar state. The Wood nymphs had also returned with the renewed foliage and Travis spotted several of them. They were teasing the dazed and severely mind-blown soldiers and some were prodding them with their spears. Travis then saw one soldier locked in a blind sexual embrace with a Wood nymph up against a tree. The soldier looked as if he was having a good, if desperate, time and was clearly unaware that his feet had turned into roots that were digging themselves into the ground.

As they walked on, Travis kept an eye out for both Prince Valerie and Sir Rodney. He never did see the Prince but they eventually came across the knight . . .

After staring at Sir Rodney for a time, Travis commented, 'Well, at least he looks happy.' Sir Rodney *did* have a dreamy smile on his face, which was just as well, all things considered. His crutches had not only taken root in the ground but were also growing into him. His hands and shoulders had merged with the wood of the crutches and there were green sprigs sprouting from the joints of his armour. A single red rose grew from the top of his helmetless head. Travis thought the effect looked quite cute. And, now that it seemed that the knight would be living out the rest of his life as a plant, Travis felt less bad about shooting both his big toes off.

'Poor fool,' was the Green Queen's only comment, before she went striding on.

They reached the edge of Mytherious Wood and stopped. A short distance from the edge sat Damion in his chair. There were four frightened-looking soldiers with him. A lot of riderless horses grazed contentedly all around them. Damion looked even worse than he had before. He was bone white and seemed completely drained. When he saw the pair of them he hissed, 'You . . . you *fiends*! How did you do it? How did you defeat my horde of monsters? They were unstoppable!'

'You pathetic *boy*,' sneered the Green Queen. 'How could you have thought that your puny powers could have threatened *me*, the Queen of Mytherious Wood?'

'Yes, Damion,' said Travis, 'you need to go back to college and take a refresher course in sorcery.'

Damion swivelled his one good eye straight at Travis's. He *really* didn't seem to be a very happy young man.

'It was *you* who provided the Green Queen with the advantage that tipped the scales in her favour,' he accused, pointing a now bony finger to Travis. 'Somehow you helped her to defeat my forces! Admit it!'

'I helped her a bit,' said Travis, beginning to feel nervous. Could Damion still present a danger?

'Sooner or later I will settle the score with you, I swear it!' snarled Damion.

Travis decided to go for the fake bravado approach and shrugged his shoulders. 'I'll make a note in my diary. Any day but Monday. I'm not a Monday person.'

'Where is Prince Valerie? What has happened to my master?' called Damion.

'With any luck he should be a sturdy pine tree by now,' Travis told him. 'Hopefully someone will eventually cut him down and turn him into a nice chest of drawers.'

'If he is still within the Wood,' said the Green Queen, 'your master will not be coming out. Ever.'

Damion shook his head. 'No, you could not have put him under your spell. My master is too powerful.'

'Of all people, *you* should appreciate what I and my Wood are capable of. You are the one who has forfeited everything to me. Be grateful I leave you with your miserable life.'

'Hah! You cannot harm me,' sneered Damion. 'I am not in your damned Wood.'

'Not *yet*,' said the Green Queen and struck her staff on the ground. Immediately green tendrils began to extend out from the edge of the Wood towards Damion.

At this the four nervous-looking soldiers turned and bolted for the hills. 'Come back, you cowards!' yelled Damion. 'You can't leave me here!' But the running soldiers kept on running. Damion stared at the advancing greenery, then screamed, 'Alright! You win! I throw myself on your mercy . . . Your Highness!'

She struck her staff again on the ground and the tendrils came to a halt. 'Then I shall let you go free,' she told Damion. 'But if you ever dare to challenge me again I will not be so merciful.'

Damion bowed his head. 'Thank you, Your Highness,' he said meekly.

The Green Queen took Travis's hand. 'Come, Travis. We shall return to my palace . . .' They rose into the air.

'Wait!' cried Damion. 'You can't just leave me here! My men have deserted me and I can't walk!'

'Tough shit,' said the Green Queen.

'Hang on,' said Travis, 'I think we should at least send someone back to help him get on a horse.'

'You do?' asked the Queen, looking surprised.

'Yes. And I know just the person.'

'Who?'

'Sharon. She and Damion used to be very close.'

'The succubus?' cried Damion in alarm. 'No! Anyone but her!'

The Green Queen smiled. 'Good choice,' she told Travis. 'Now hold tight.' And off they flew, Damion's hysterical pleas receding into the background.

Chapter Twenty-Four

'He's nowhere in the Wood,' said the Green Queen. 'I don't know how, but he must have got away.'

It was late in the day and they were standing by the Queen's magic pool. Through it they had scanned every inch of Mytherious Wood for Prince Valerie, or even a tree-shaped Prince Valerie, but had found no trace of him. The Wood nymphs had been quizzed and though some remembered seeing the Prince, none knew what had happened to him.

'Maybe he just turned himself into a bat and flew away,' suggested Travis. 'That's one of the advantages of being a vampire.'

'I won't ever feel safe now,' said Beatrice.

'You can stay here with me, child,' the Green Queen told her. 'Within the Wood you'll always be safe.'

'Thank you, Your Highness.'

'Can I stay too?' asked Annabelle, shyly. 'It's not just because I'm frightened of the Prince. I . . . I want to become a Wood nymph. If you'll have me, Your Highness.'

The Green Queen patted her on the shoulder. 'Of course you may stay, Annabelle. And I think you'd make a delightful Wood nymph.'

Travis looked at Sharon. 'And what about you?' he asked hopefully. 'Would you like to stay and become a Wood nymph too?'

Sharon's response was to roll her eyes and stick her tongue out at him.

'I was afraid you'd say that,' he sighed.

'What about me?' said Jack. 'Can I stay?'

'*You* want to become a Wood nymph?' asked Travis.

'Nah. I just want to stay here. This is my kind of place.' He glanced unhappily at Sharon. 'Sorry, babe, but I like being a human being again. And Prenderghast can't touch me here either.'

'Out of the question, I'm afraid,' said the Green Queen firmly. 'Mortal men cannot remain here indefinitely, only for short periods as my guests.'

'Shit,' muttered Jack. Then to Sharon, 'Well, babe, looks like we're an item again.'

'Up yours,' she told him.

Travis felt disappointed, though he hadn't really thought that he was going to escape Jack's company so easily. But looking on the bright side, he had unloaded two responsibilities: Annabelle and Beatrice. He would miss them both, especially Beatrice, infuriating, stuck-up little twit that she was much of the time. That just left him with Jack and Sharon. He gave the succubus a slightly nervous glance. She still hadn't told him what she'd done to Damion. She'd been under strict instructions from the Green Queen not to kill the sorcerer but the evil smirk on her face when she'd returned convinced Travis that she had exacted an extremely unpleasant revenge.

'Now it's my turn to keep to the letter of our bargain,' said the Green Queen.

Distracted, Travis suddenly realized she was addressing him. 'Pardon? Bargain?'

'The one we made last night,' she told him with a smile. 'Surely you haven't forgotten?'

He felt his cheeks redden. All four of them. 'Oh yes. You're going to tell me where to find the Key.'

'So I believe. First, travel to the city of Lankhair. It's ten days ride from here. Follow the road that lies to the north of the Wood. When you arrive at Lankhair, find a street called the Knobbly Way then go to number twelve and ask the man who dwells there about the Key.'

Travis nodded. 'Number twelve . . . Knobbly Way, Lankhair . . . on the road north. I've got it.' It all seemed terribly mundane. 'You really think this guy will know where the Key is?'

'Trust me,' said the Green Queen, and winked at him.

*

'Hurry up,' said Sharon.

'Hold your horses. I'm doing my best,' said Travis, as he tried to finish buckling up his saddle. Whiplash, as always, was no help and kept fidgeting. Sharon, already astride her own horse, was looking like some feral Lady Godiva in the early morning light. Jack sulked nearby. Understandably, he wasn't looking forward to leaving Mytherious Wood.

'Wait for me!'

Travis turned. Beatrice was leading her horse from the Palace, dressed once again in her travelling clothes. 'Where do you think you're going?' he asked her.

'I'm coming with you, silly,' she told him.

'What? But you said you wanted to stay here! Where you'll be safe . . .'

'I've done a lot of serious thinking since then,' she said.

Travis stifled the urge to laugh. Beatrice and serious thinking seemed mutually exclusive concepts. 'And?'

'I decided I didn't want to stay here. Oh, it's a wonderful place and I love the Green Queen – I'm one of her *worshippers* for goodness sake! – and I'm still terrified of Prince Valerie, but to stay here for the rest of my life would be admitting defeat. I'm not going to let the Prince cower me in this way. Do you see?'

'I guess so,' Travis said reluctantly. He had mixed feelings about her decision. One side of him was happy to have the continued pleasure of her company, his other side groaned at the thought of continuing to be responsible for her. 'But are you absolutely sure about his?'

'Yes, I am,' she said firmly. 'I've explained everything to the Green Queen and she quite understands. She gave me her blessing.'

'That'll come in handy,' Travis muttered. 'Oh well, welcome back on board.' He finished the last buckle and mounted Whiplash. Then he helped Jack climb up behind him. Jack and Sharon were still not speaking. Or rather Sharon wasn't speaking to Jack. Jack gave a long sigh. 'I'm going to miss being me.'

'Well, when I get the Key maybe we can settle things for good with Prenderghast,' Travis said.

'Yeah, and pigs will get free airplane tickets,' said Jack bitterly.

Travis said nothing. Then, when Beatrice had mounted her horse, he turned to the Palace and raised his arm in salute. He had said his goodbyes to the Green Queen earlier but knew she would be watching. Then he began to lead his little party out of Mytherious Wood.

When they reached the very edge of the Wood Travis brought Whiplash to a halt. 'Are you ready?' he asked Jack over his shoulder.

'Yeah,' said Jack, reluctantly, 'let's get it over with . . .'

Travis urged the horse forward. The moment they emerged from the Wood Travis felt Jack's grip around his waist vanish. Then he heard the familiar fluttering of leathery wings and Jack, a demon once more, landed on the horse's head. 'I was kinda hoping the Green babe might have got her wires crossed about this,' he said to Travis.

'I'm sorry,' said Travis.

'Well, I got to look on the bright side . . .' He took out his pack of Marlboro and lit up, 'I'm out of the non-smoking zone, and I could *murder* a dish of goats' testicle stew.'

It used to be said of Wardour Street, the thoroughfare in London's Soho where Britain's film companies were once based, that it was the only existing street that was shady on both sides. The streets of Lankhair were not only shady on both sides but also in the middle. This was because their narrowness was compounded by the ramshackle wooden buildings on either side which leaned so precariously forward their roofs touched. A glimpse of the sky anywhere in Lankhair was therefore a cause of great excitement.

Lankhair, Travis had learned – apart from being a dirty, gloomy, rat-ridden slum of a town – was a centre for all kinds of shady dealings. It was a magnet for every devious, shifty, manipulating con-man on Samella. No wonder that Jack seemed quite at home.

'Here it is, number twelve,' announced Jack, from the top of Whiplash's head.

'I'll take your word for it,' said Travis, peering into the gloom. He could vaguely make out some sort of shop front. Jack snapped his fingers, producing a small ball of fire. It cast a red glow on the building, allowing Travis to see a hanging sign over the front door which said 'Ye Olde Quest Shoppe.'

'This must be the place,' said Travis, and dismounted. Beatrice and Sharon did likewise. Passersby paid them no attention. Lankhair was a place where it was wise to mind your own business. They tied the horses up to a hitching rail then Travis went and banged the door knocker.

After a wait of nearly a minute the door creaked open. An old man, wearing a long and dusty red coat, who could have made a fortune playing Santa Claus in department stores looked them up and down, gave them a beaming smile and said, 'Don't tell me it's Halloween again already!'

'What?' said Travis.

'Just my little joke. Come in . . . come in . . .' He opened the door wider, stepped aside and ushered them in. Travis looked around curiously. The interior of the shop was more like that of a warehouse. A very untidy and very dusty warehouse. Boxes, crates and elaborate chests were piled on top of each other in all directions. There were great banks of wooden drawers, none of which appeared to be indexed in any way. How the old man managed to find anything in the place was a mystery.

'My name is Best. Jeremy P. Best,' the old man told them. 'And you kind people are . . . ?'

Travis made the introductions then said, 'We were told you might be able to help me find something. Something special.'

Best flashed his beaming smile again and chuckled. 'Finding special things for people is my speciality. As you can see.' He spread his arms wide to encompass the shop. Clouds of dust flew from his billowing sleeves. 'My motto is: "Forget the Quest – go straight to Best." '

'You collect things then?' asked Travis, trying not to sneeze.

'In a manner of speaking. But not just any old thing – only *special* things,' said Best proudly. 'The things that quests are made of.'

'Let me get this straight, granpa,' said Jack, 'You've got some sort of racket where you go on quests on behalf of other people?'

'Not me personally,' said Best, 'I hire suitable types to do the questing for me – disgraced knights, out-of-work adventurers, clapped-out barbarians, alcoholic ex-tax inspectors, types who are willing to take incredible risks for a bit of cash in the hand. Of course, they're not always successful but I reckon to win more than I lose.'

'And when people genuinely need the things your mercenaries find, they have to come to you, right?' asked Travis.

Best nodded eagerly.

'And then you charge them an arm and a leg and probably some major vital organ, I'll bet,' added Jack.

'I'd prefer to say we usually come to a mutually satisfying arrangement,' said Best smoothly.

Travis decided that Best's Santa Clause-like appearance was very deceptive. He hoped there was enough gold left in Prince Valerie's purse to pay the little crook's finder's fee, should Best actually possess the Key.

'Now how can I help you?' beamed Best. 'Looking for a magic sword? A magic ring? A magic amulet that will revive the forces of Good in your stricken kingdom? A special seal that will help you regain your throne? Am I getting warm?'

'None of those things,' Travis told him. 'I'm looking for something called the Key. Though I don't know if it actually *is* a key. To be honest, I don't know what it is exactly.'

Best put a finger to his lips and frowned. ' "The Key" . . . hmmm, and your name – Travis Thomson – seems to ring a bell somewhere.' He frowned harder, then suddenly beamed and exclaimed, 'Ahah!' Then he bustled over to a towering chest of drawers and pulled out the bottom one. He bent down and started tossing keys of all shapes and sizes onto the floor. 'No . . . no . . . no . . . no . . .' he muttered as he tossed out the keys. Then he said 'Ahah!' again and stood up. 'I thought so . . . ' he beamed in a way that Travis was swiftly finding deeply irritating. He came back to Travis and held out his hand.

Travis saw that he had an old fashioned silver key about four inches long. Tied to it with a red ribbon was a large white cardboard tag. On the tag was written, in a flourishing hand, 'THE KEY – FOR THE USE OF TRAVIS THOMSON EXCLUSIVELY.'

'The Key *is* a key?' said Travis, not really daring to believe things were that simple.

'So it would seem,' said Best, beaming.

Travis reached out to take it but Best closed his hand, 'Now we must talk business.' He was no longer beaming.

Travis sighed.'How much?'

'One hundred sovereigns,' said Best quickly, then added, 'I have high overheads.'

'Can I ask a question, granpa?' asked Jack.

'Be my guest,' said Best.

'We outnumber you. What's to prevent us just grabbing the damn thing and dumping you in one of your drawers?'

Best made a little whistling sound. There was a rustling sound from above, accompanied by a fall of dust. Travis looked up. In the blackness beyond the beams and rafters that criss-crossed the ceiling something was stirring. He glimpsed a single red eye slowly opening. And ten great tentacles began menacingly to descend . . .

'Good answer,' said Jack to Best.

Best whistled again. The tentacles stopped, then began to slowly retract. 'That's Oscar,' said Best, beaming. 'He's my protector and debt collector.'

Travis took out the Prince's purse and emptied its contents into his hand. He counted the coins. 'I was afraid so. Only forty sovereigns left . . . shit.'

'No deal then,' said Best. 'Come back when you've got the full amount.'

Travis groaned. 'Where the hell am I going to find another sixty sovereigns?'

'On me,' said Beatrice and produced a bulging purse from one of her pockets.

Travis took it and looked inside. It was full of gold coins. 'Where did you get this?' he asked in amazement.

'From the Green Queen. She thought you might be a little short.'

'That woman is a goddess!' cried Travis eagerly counting out sovereigns.

'We *know* that, Travis,' said Beatrice.

Travis paid Best the hundred sovereigns and then took the Key. He gazed at it reverently. 'Okay, so I've got the Key, but what do I do with it?'

No one had an answer. Finally Jack said, 'Why don't you try wishing on it?'

'Wishing?'

'Yeah. Try wishing yourself back home. And if it works don't forget to put in a good word for me when you see Prenderghast again.'

'I really don't think it can be that simple . . .' said Travis, but to himself he wished, 'I want to go back home!'

Travis woke up. His radio-alarm clock had switched itself on and he could hear Kylie Minogue singing 'I Should Be So Lucky!' No doubt someone's idea of a sick joke. He sat up and looked around. He was in his own bedroom. Then he looked at the clock. It was 8 a.m. And the date was the thirteenth of January. He looked down at himself. He was wearing his 'Wasp Factory' tee-shirt and green y-fronts. Then he became aware that he had a terrible headache.

Carefully, he got out of bed and went to the window. He pulled the curtains open. St John's Wood, in all its grotty splendour, lay spread out before him. He was definitely back.

He sat down on the bed. Back from where? Already his memories of Samella had taken on the stuff of dreams. Had it all been the result of an over-strong curry? Or too much wine? He remembered the Indian restaurant he'd been to with Heather the night before. Or did he? Had that been part of the dream too?

What the hell. Whatever had happened to him, it was all over now.

He heard his toilet flush.

He frowned. Had Heather come back with him? Unusual

for her to do that on a week day. He got up and opened his bedroom door. At that moment the bathroom door opened and a naked woman came out.

Sharon.

She smiled at him. 'Feeling better?'

'Gah . . .' replied Travis.

'Good,' she said and disappeared into the kitchen. On shaky legs he followed her. In the kitchen, and wearing his dressing gown, was Beatrice. She was sitting at the table and eating a piece of toast. 'Hello, Travis,' she greeted him brightly, then went back to watching breakfast TV on his portable black and white set.

'Gah . . .' he replied.

Perched on top of the refrigerator was Jack. He had a cup of coffee in one hand and a Marlboro in the other. 'You look worse than the make-up job we did on the creature in *Hell-Sucker from Jupiter*,' Jack told him cheerfully. Then he too returned his attention to the TV. 'You know you can only get four channels on that thing?' he said.

'Gah . . .' said Travis. He looked around for Whiplash. Thankfully, the horse was nowhere to be seen. But that didn't mean he wasn't standing outside in Travis's parking space.

Sharon, who somehow managed to look even more naked in his kitchen than she had back on Samella, was at the sink, filling his electric kettle. 'Want some coffee, Travis?' she asked. 'Jack has shown us how everything works. It's fun here!'

Travis fell into a chair. 'Gah . . .' Then he tried again. 'What . . . are you all doing here?'

'Beats me, boss,' said Jack with a shrug. 'One moment we're in that shyster's shop and the next we're in your living room. You passed out and we put you to bed.'

'But you *can't* be here! You're not real! You're just characters from a weird dream . . .'

Beatrice took another precise bite from her piece of toast and said dismissively, 'Don't be silly, Travis.'

'I figure that Prenderghast hasn't finished with you yet,' said Jack. 'Or me.'

And then the doorbell rang.